P9-BYM-959

THE CASE OF THE MISSING DINOSAUR EGG

The First Kids Mysteries

The Case of the Rock 'n' Roll Dog

The Case of the Diamond Dog Collar

The Case of the Ruby Slippers

The Case of the Piggy Bank Thief

The Case of the Missing Dinosaur Egg

THE CASE OF THE MISSING DINOSAUR EGG

MARTHA FREEMAN

Holiday House / New York

HOLIDAY HOUSE is registered in the U.S. Patent and Trademark Office.
Printed and Bound in January 2013 at Maple Press, York, PA, USA.
First Edition
1 3 5 7 9 10 8 6 4 2
www.holidayhouse.com

Library of Congress Cataloging-in-Publication Data

Freeman, Martha, 1956-
The case of the missing dinosaur egg / by Martha Freeman.—1st ed.
p. cm. — (First kids mystery ; #5)
Summary: Seven-year-old Tessa and ten-year-old Cammie, daughters of the first female president, and their dog Hooligan, investigate when an ostrich egg is substituted for a rare dinosaur egg on loan from another country.
ISBN 978-0-8234-2523-5
1. White House (Washington, D.C.)—Juvenile fiction. [1. White House (Washington, D.C.)—Fiction. 2. Presidents—Family—Fiction. 3. Sisters—Fiction. 4. Dogs—Fiction. 5. Lost and found possessions—Fiction. 6. Washington (D.C.)—Fiction. 7. Mystery and detective stories.] I. Title.
PZ7.F87496Cap 2013
[Fic]—dc23

2012033735

For Professor Ann Marie Major,
in gratitude for her friendship,
her expertise and her students.

CHARACTERS

Cameron Parks (Cammie), our narrator, is the ten-year-old daughter of U.S. president Marilee Parks and her husband, Rick. Since Cameron's mom was inaugurated in January, she has lived in the White House with her extended family.

Tessa Parks, Cameron's sister, is seven years old and a drama queen.

Nathan Leone (Nate) is Cameron and Tessa's cousin, the only child of their aunt Jen. Nate was born in Korea. Aunt Jen adopted him as an infant and brought him to live with her in San Diego. Now he and Aunt Jen live with Tessa and Cameron's family in the White House.

Jennifer Maclaren Leone (Aunt Jen) is Cameron and Tessa's aunt and Nate's mom. A widow, she lives with Nate in an apartment on the third floor of the

White House and acts as First Lady in President Parks's administration. President Parks is her younger sister.

Jeremy, Charlotte and Malik are Secret Service agents who help keep the First Family safe.

Mr. Morgan and Mr. Webb are security officers with the Smithsonian Institution. Previously, they helped Tessa, Cameron and Nate solve the Case of the Ruby Slippers.

Barbara Maclaren (Granny, aka Judge Maclaren) is Cameron, Tessa and Nate's grandmother. She used to be a judge in California, and before that a district attorney, and before that a police officer. When Cameron and Tessa's mom won the presidential election, Granny agreed to come to Washington to help take care of Cameron, Tessa and Nate.

Willis Bryant is Granny's special friend. He used to run the White House elevator but now works for Cameron's family, taking care of their too-energetic dog, Hooligan, on weekdays.

Jan and Larry (she's blond, he's not) are popular local newscasters in Greater Metropolitan Washington.

Marilee Maclaren Parks (Mom) is Cameron and Tessa's mom and, since January, the president of the United States. She's a lawyer, and she used to be a senator from California.

✖

Rick Parks (Dad) is Cameron and Tessa's dad. He has a job building airplanes in California, so he is usually in Washington only on weekends. He used to be an air force pilot.

Mr. Brackbill is the librarian at Cameron, Tessa and Nate's school.

Evgenia is in Cameron and Nate's fifth-grade class. She is very smart and quiet.

Hooligan is Cameron and Tessa's dog. He looks like a Dr. Seuss version of an Afghan hound. "Hooligan" is a word that means rowdy, but Hooligan is not really bad. He just has too much energy.

Ms. Ann Major is a deputy assistant press secretary in the office of President Parks. Her beagle, Pickles, has playdates with First Dog Hooligan.

Antonia Alfredo-Chin (Toni) is a friend of Cameron, Tessa and Nate's who also happens to be the niece of the president of a certain nearby nation and the daughter of its ambassador to the United States. She lives in Washington, D.C. Her dog, Ozzabelle, was a gift from Tessa and Cameron.

CHAPTER ONE

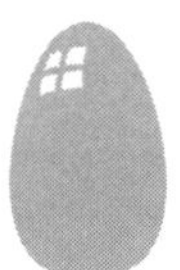

My little sister, Tessa, leaned over and whispered in my ear, "That is the biggest egg I ever saw."

True, it was a really big egg. But we were in the audience at a talk at a museum, and we were supposed to be quiet. I shushed my sister, but she ignored me.

"It makes sense, though, doesn't it, Cammie?" Tessa said. "Dinosaurs were big. So their babies were big. A big baby needs a big egg."

Now my cousin Nate joined in. "They're called hatchlings, not babies, Tessa." Nate is ten like me. Tessa is seven.

Nate's mom looked over at us, put her finger to her lips and nodded at the man who was talking. On the table in front of him was the gleaming, cream-colored egg.

I pointed at myself and shrugged, meaning *Me? I didn't do anything!*, which made Nate's mom—my aunt Jen—frown.

Oh, fine.

It was a Saturday afternoon in April, the week before Easter. Outside, it was a beautiful day. We live in Washington, D.C., and down by the Tidal Basin the cherry trees were blossoming. What I really wanted to do was go play outside with my dog, but instead I was cooped up with a bunch of ancient bones and grown-ups at the National Museum of Natural History.

Don't get me wrong. I like the museum, and I like dinosaurs. But when you're the kid of the president of the United States, like I am, you spend a little too much time being quiet and polite.

With no choice, I shook the wiggles out of my shoulders, resettled my posterior into the chair and tried to listen. The speaker's name was Professor Cordell Bohn, and he was a paleontologist—pronounced "pay-lee-un-TALL-uh-jist" —which is a person who studies long-ago plants and animals, like dinosaurs.

"Most people are surprised to learn that fossilized dinosaur eggs are reasonably common in many locations around the world," Professor Bohn was saying. "What's unique in this case, uh... unique—"

Professor Bohn stopped, looked down at the egg and raised his eyebrows. Was he listening to something?

A few seconds passed, nothing happened and Professor Bohn tried again.

"As I was saying, this find may help us better understand the link between dinosaurs and modern-day birds. We are hoping to study the shell—"

He stopped again, and this time everybody heard it—*rata-tap-tap-tap* coming from the egg.

What the heck?

Somebody gasped; other people whispered and pointed. Professor Bohn himself took a step backward but at the same time said, "There is no cause for alarm."

Meanwhile, my little sister leaned over. "Cammie? Is it going to hatch?"

Nate answered before I could. "Don't be ridiculous. Dinosaurs have been extinct for sixty-five million years."

Extinct or not, the *rata-tap* continued, and now the egg began to wobble!

To the left of me, a man wearing an untucked white shirt and black dress pants jumped up, ready to run. Next thing, the people beside him did the same; then . . . *rata-tata-tap . . . rata-tata-TAP . . . rata-tata-CRACK!* The eggshell broke and—right before our eyes—something damp, gray and funny-looking started to bust out!

CHAPTER TWO

"Gangway!" someone shouted, and a lot of people headed for the exits.

Meanwhile, a lady from the museum cried, "Ladies and gentlemen! Please exit in an orderly manner!"

Exit? Who wanted to exit? I wanted to see what was in that egg! But then my little sister sprang up, and of course I had to comfort her. "Don't worry, Tessa. It's much too small to hurt us."

"I know that—*duh*. I just want a closer look!" And—before Aunt Jen or the Secret Service could stop her—Tessa started climbing over chairs to get to the front of the room.

Aunt Jen sputtered, "Oh, for Pete's sake!" and climbed after Tessa, except Aunt Jen was wearing a narrow skirt and high heels, so navigating chairs was maybe not her most graceful maneuver. Nate and I tried not to laugh as she tripped and stumbled forward, but in the confusion, I was pretty sure no one else even noticed.

Meanwhile, I wished I could see what the egg was doing, but there were too many bodies in front of me.

"Jeremy!" I looked around for the tallest Secret Service agent. "Can you see?"

Jeremy stood on tiptoes. "Looks like the little fella's making progress," he said. "There's part of its head and maybe a shoulder . . . er, if it's even got shoulders."

"Does it have a crest—can you see?" Nate wanted to know. "Like a velociraptor?"

"What about huge, deadly teeth?" I asked. "Like T. rex?"

Jeremy shook his head. "Hard to tell from here. But if I had to guess, I'd say it had a beak and damp little feathers."

Nate nodded. "That makes sense. The latest research indicates many dinosaurs did have feathers."

I said, "Wait—I thought according to you it couldn't be a dinosaur."

My cousin shrugged. "It's a dinosaur egg, isn't it?"

Over all the noise in the room, I heard something new—laughter, which turned out to be Professor Bohn's.

"Ladies and gentlemen," he said, "if I can reclaim your attention? I'm afraid those of you hoping for something prehistoric are going to be disappointed. On the other hand, you could call this chick a modern-day dinosaur."

Nate grabbed my arm. "Come on. Let's get closer to the action."

Jeremy followed us as we made our way through the crowd. Soon we could see the chick's busy beak, chipping away at its prison, and pieces of white shell littering the floor and table.

"Hey," I said when I finally got a good look. "I've got a book about birds at home. Isn't that an ostrich?"

Professor Bohn heard me and nodded. "Very good, Cameron."

"I knew that," said Nate quickly.

Tessa shook her head. "Wow—nature is sure awesome! Who'd've thought an ostrich could come out of a dinosaur egg?"

Professor Bohn made a face that meant he was trying not to smile. "Well, actually, Tessa, the truth is this egg never belonged to a dinosaur. Dinosaur eggs, as you'll see when you tour the rest of the exhibit, are fossilized and look like rocks."

Aunt Jen said, "In that case, you must have known this egg belonged to a bird. Why didn't you say anything?"

Professor Bohn looked down at his shoes. "My bad." Then he looked up, and I noticed there were lots of laugh crinkles around his eyes. "I have a soft spot for pranks, and it was obvious to me that's what this was. I didn't want to spoil the fun, so I'm afraid I asked the museum staff if we could wait and see how it played out."

My aunt does not have what you'd call a big sense of humor. Without smiling, she nodded and said, "Ah."

Meanwhile, Nate asked, "Where's the real dinosaur egg?"

Professor Bohn started to answer, but the lady from

the museum beat him to it. "Nothing to worry about. We have the case well in hand."

"Case?" Tessa perked up. "Are you saying there's a mystery?"

"Oh, no, no, no." The lady shook her head. "It's not a mystery at all. The egg has, uh...just been misplaced. I'm sure it will turn up soon."

CHAPTER THREE

Tessa folded her arms across her chest and frowned. "Well, *that's* disappointing." The other grown-ups all looked super serious, but Professor Bohn laughed.

I was beginning to think I liked Professor Bohn.

Also, I knew what Tessa was thinking. She wanted a new mystery for us to solve! Since January, when Mom got to be president and our family moved into the White House, Nate, Tessa and I have investigated four different cases—and we've even been on the news.

By now we could see the ostrich chick's head—big beady eyes and a fierce-looking beak at the top of a long spotted neck. Honestly? It was ugly. But I remembered one time we had chicken eggs hatch in my class at school. The chicks started off disgusting, but then they dried off, fluffed up and got cute.

Tessa must have had the same idea, because she said, trying to sound casual about it, "So, who gets to keep the ostrich?"

"Oh, no." Aunt Jen shook her head. "Unh-unh, Tessa. Not happening."

Tessa said, *"Ple-e-ease,"* Aunt Jen said, *"No-o-o,"* and finally a guy in a blue shirt explained it would take the chick hours to get out of its egg, and then it would need to be washed in special soap to kill germs, and after that it would have to live in a special kind of electric box for a few days while it got used to life in the world.

"As it's growing up, it needs a pen and the company of other chicks," he said. "Plus there's one more thing. About half of ostrich chicks die... even if you do everything right."

My sister looked horrified.

Aunt Jen said, "You seem to know a lot about ostriches."

The man smiled and said he worked at the National Zoo. "We don't have ostriches," he said, "but we have rheas and emus, which are also ratites—big birds that don't fly."

Aunt Jen looked at Tessa. "Since the zoo has the equipment to raise a chick, why don't we let them take care of this guy? Then when he's bigger, you can go visit."

Tessa sighed. "I guess, but can we name him, at least?"

"What did you have in mind?" Aunt Jen asked.

"Uh..." Tessa looked at me. "Cammie, you do it."

I grinned. "Isn't it obvious? Dino!"

By this time, almost everyone had left the lecture room. Some of them were probably still running for their lives, but the rest were looking at the dinosaur egg exhibit, which was down a hallway. Professor Bohn said he didn't mind losing his audience. Nothing he had been planning to say was as exciting as watching a dinosaur egg hatch.

"Since we're finished here, would you kids like to take a quick tour of the exhibit?" Professor Bohn asked us.

We kids never had a chance to answer. Aunt Jen did it for us: "They would *love* to."

CHAPTER FOUR

Professor Bohn led us to the exhibit hall, where a sign over the doorway read: CRACKING UP: THE INNER LIVES OF DINOSAUR EGGS.

We went in. Along one wall there were windows looking onto 3-D scenes of mama dinosaurs taking care of eggs and hatchlings. In the middle of the room were glass cases containing real fossilized eggs and the fossils of young dinosaurs. A few contained fossils of broken eggs with the bones of never-hatched hatchlings inside.

Poor hatchlings.

The reason the fossils look like rocks, Professor Bohn explained, is simple: They *are* rocks. An egg fossil is made when an egg gets buried in sand and the sand gets flooded with water. Over millions of years, minerals in the water mix with minerals in the eggshell and form rock.

Here are some more things I learned about dinosaur eggs that day:

- Dinosaur nests have been found at more than two hundred sites around the world.
- In Montana, a whole lot have been found that were made by a kind of dinosaur that took really good care of its hatchlings.
- Most dinosaurs buried their eggs in leaves, grass or dirt to keep them warm and safe.
- The biggest dinosaur eggs are about two feet long, and the smallest are about the size of goose eggs.

It's true I started the afternoon with a bad attitude, but the stuff Professor Bohn told us was pretty cool—especially what he told us last.

"The more we learn about dinosaurs, the more we find out how much they're like birds," he said. "They apparently had feathers—"

"I knew that," Nate said.

"—and their eggs and bodily structure are also avian, which means birdlike. In fact, some scientists believe birds and dinosaurs are the same type of animals and shouldn't be considered separate at all."

By then it was time for us to leave the museum.

"What did you think of the exhibit, kids?" a reporter called as we walked through the rotunda. That's the big round room at the front where there's a huge stuffed African bull elephant.

Nate and I smiled, gave thumbs-up signs and kept walking.

But Tessa stopped, which—as usual—caused all the photographers in the room to go crazy snapping pictures. "We saw a dinosaur hatch," she said. "It was so-o-o cool!"

The reporter scribbled something, and a lot of people laughed. Aunt Jen said, "A dinosaur, Tessa? Or an ostrich?"

"Same thing!" Tessa said. "That's what Professor Bohn told us."

This led to more questions, and Tessa would happily have stayed all day, explaining and having her picture taken, but Aunt Jen thanked the news guys and shooed us forward. Meanwhile, Professor Bohn and the woman from the museum hung back and took questions. The woman was a paleontologist, too: Professor Teresa Rexington. She and Professor Bohn and a team of scientists from a certain nearby nation had found the dinosaur egg fossil that was now missing.

Our van was parked outside at the curb. We were about to climb in for the short ride home when I noticed two familiar men on their way up the steps to the museum. Among all those people wearing jeans and T-shirts, they stood out because they were wearing suits.

Nate had seen them, too, and he nudged me. "Cammie, isn't that—"

"Mr. Morgan and Mr. Webb!" I waved. "Hey, hi! How are you?"

Mr. Morgan and Mr. Webb are security guys for the Smithsonian. Now they came over to the van and nodded hello. Neither of them smiles much, and Mr. Webb hardly even talks.

Tessa got right to the point. "Are you here to investigate the missing egg? It's okay"—she winked—"you can tell us."

Mr. Morgan made sure no one was listening before he answered: "In fact, we may need to ask for your help. From what we've been told, the situation is, uh . . . complicated."

Tessa pumped her fist. "*Woot*—I knew it! The First Kids are back on the job!"

CHAPTER FIVE

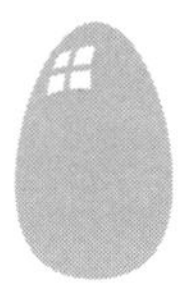

Or were we?

All the rest of that day, we waited for a call...but none came.

I did get my wish to play with our big furry mutt, Hooligan, outside on the South Lawn. Nate practiced piano—did I mention he is some kind of piano genius? And Tessa cleaned up after the stray cat and kittens we found a couple of weeks ago near the Rose Garden. They live mostly in a box in Hooligan's room, which is two doors down from ours on the White House second floor.

Tessa and I ate dinner with Granny and her special friend, Mr. Bryant. Nate ate with his mom in their apartment on the third floor. After Mr. Bryant went home, Tessa, Nate and I played a few hands of hearts with Granny in the solarium, which is kind of like our rec room.

Finally, Granny announced it was time for bed, but

Tessa wanted to stay up and watch Jan and Larry, our favorite TV newscasters.

"Maybe the dinosaur exhibit will be on," Tessa said.

"You just want to see if *you're* on," Nate said.

Tessa didn't disagree, and Granny said, "Okay, five more minutes."

Nate grabbed the remote, turned on the TV and...

Uh-oh.

What we saw wasn't Tessa or a dinosaur egg; it was Aunt Jen's posterior as she hurdled and climbed over chair backs! At least the only visible underwear was her slip's lacy hem. Watching it, Nate was so embarrassed he had to close his eyes.

On TV, Larry tried to sound serious: "...First Auntie Jennifer Leone making a heroic attempt to catch First Daughter Tessa Parks at the National Museum of Natural History today...," while in the background Jan was giggling so hard she hiccupped.

After that, the view switched to some egg fossils, Nate and me doing the thumbs-up and Tessa saying we'd seen a dinosaur hatch.

Then Professor Bohn and the paleontologist from the museum, Professor Rexington, explained a little about birds and dinosaurs.

Finally, Jan said, "On a more serious note, Larry, unnamed sources tell us tonight that one of the dinosaur eggs from the exhibit has gone missing." The screen showed a picture of the missing egg, which sure enough, looked like a gray, egg-shaped rock. "And because the egg was a rare specimen excavated at a site in a certain nearby nation, its disappearance could have international political implications."

Larry cut in: "You mean this story is no yolk, Jan?"

Jan rolled her eyes. "You're hilarious, Larry."

After that they cut to a commercial, Granny said, "Bedtime," and Nate turned off the TV.

A ramp leads from the solarium down to the White House third floor. Walking down it, I asked Granny if she knew what Jan and Larry had meant about the missing egg having "international political implications."

Granny shrugged. "Try asking your parents," she said. "It's a mystery to me."

One thing about having your mom be president of the United States—you don't get to see her all the time. That Saturday evening, she and Dad had to go to some dinner thing. Tessa and I were in bed reading when they came in to say good night.

"Mama!" Tessa said. "I need a snuggle! Hi, Daddy! Explain about the dinosaur egg, please. Granny said you could."

Mom sat down on the edge of Tessa's bed, and Dad sat down on the edge of mine. The White House has tons of bedrooms, but we share because when we first moved in, neither one of us wanted to sleep alone.

"What dinosaur egg?" Dad asked. He was wearing a tuxedo, and Mom had on a dark-red dress and white beads.

Tessa told them how one was missing from the museum, and Mom said, "Oh, dear, muffin—it's complicated." She looked at Dad.

He closed his eyes, yawned and nodded all at the same time. "I guess there's a legend in this certain nearby nation that no life existed there in prehistoric times—not even dinosaurs. Supposedly, the first life didn't come until much later, when a heroic leader arrived and founded a city. After that came llamas and pyramids and cocoa beans and...well, you get the idea."

Tessa shook her head. "No, I don't."

But I thought I understood. "Jan and Larry said the egg was found in a certain nearby nation, right? So if that's true, the legend is wrong. There must've been dinosaurs there after all."

Tessa shrugged. "Oh, okay. But big whoop."

"Big whoop," Mom repeated, "unless you're the president of the certain nearby nation and you claim to be the great-great-and-so-on-grandson of the heroic leader. In fact, you claim that's one reason you're entitled to be president in perpetuity."

"What's per-pe-whatever you said?" Tessa wanted to know.

"Forever," Dad said. "In other words, instead of having elections and somebody new getting to be president, you just stay president."

Tessa looked horrified. "Oh, *no*! You don't want to do that, Mama, do you?"

Mom looked tired. "Not tonight, I don't."

"But wait a second," I said. "The president of the certain nearby nation is Manfred Alfredo-Chin, right? Whose dog is Hooligan's friend? Whose niece is our friend, Toni?"

Dad nodded. "That's the guy."

"So if everybody found out the legend's wrong because now there's this dinosaur egg, it might be bad for President Alfredo-Chin," I said. "And he's already got trouble because of those protests going on in his nation."

In case you hadn't guessed, my little sister is a drama queen. Now she waved her arms the way she does. "Oh, come on! No way did President Manfred Alfredo-Chin ever steal any dinosaur egg! First, he's our friend. Second, he doesn't even live here. And third, presidents don't do stuff like that—do they, Mama?"

Mom said, "I have never personally stolen a dinosaur egg, nor, to the best of my knowledge, has anyone on my staff."

Dad rolled his eyes. "Honey? You know you're speaking to your family, right? You're not on television."

Mom smiled. "Right. Anyway, I doubt President Alfredo-Chin is responsible for the missing egg. If I had to guess, I'd say the problem is at the museum. And now, muffins . . ." She stood up and yawned. "I am going to say good night. Church tomorrow, remember? It's Palm Sunday."

CHAPTER SIX

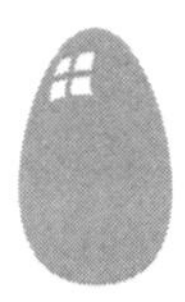

The next day started out normal...but got abnormal fast.

The normal part was Granny waking us for church at eight o'clock. But ten minutes later Charlotte knocked on Tessa's and my door while we were getting dressed. Charlotte is my favorite Secret Service agent.

"Mr. Webb and Mr. Morgan are in the Treaty Room, and they'd like to meet with you before church," she said. "Nate is on his way down."

Tessa didn't say a word—just yanked her dress over her shoulders and headed for the door.

"Shoes, Tessa?" I said. "Hair?"

"My hair's fine, and you can bring my shoes, okay? I'm in a hurry! But, oh..." She doubled back, opened her closet and grabbed a pink spangled baseball cap, the one she wears for detecting. "Don't forget your notebook!" she told me, and left.

Oh, Tessa.

I stepped into my own shoes, picked Tessa's up off the floor, got my notebook and a pen and followed.

When we first moved here, the house seemed huge—more like a hotel than a place to live. But now I'm getting used to it—paintings, chandeliers, antiques, elevators and just plain bigness everywhere.

The first floor, the State Floor, is basically a public place. Tourists come through most mornings, and there're always staff and marines around. Up here on the second and third floors, though, it's usually just the family and our guests and maybe housekeepers cleaning. Even so, it's big and fancy, and you never get away from the history.

Like now when I walked out our bedroom door? There was a window to my right at the end of the hall. It looks out over the North Portico—the front door—and it's where Abraham Lincoln stood to make his last speech.

The Treaty Room, where we were meeting Mr. Morgan and Mr. Webb, is across the Center Hall from our bedroom. Like a lot of presidents, my mom uses it as an office sometimes. There are some famous paintings in it, besides a big desk President Ulysses S. Grant used for cabinet meetings.

Now when I walked in carrying my notebook and Tessa's shoes, Mr. Webb and Mr. Morgan were sitting on a sofa holding coffee mugs, Tessa was sitting across from them in a chair and Granny and Charlotte were standing beside her. Nate wasn't there yet—no surprise. He is not a morning person.

I gave Tessa her shoes. "Granny said I can have coffee," she told me as she buckled them, "because this is a business meeting."

Coffee tastes terrible, but no way would I let my little sister out-grown-up me. "Can I, too?" I asked.

Granny said, "Yes you *may*," and rang for Mr. Patel, the cutest White House butler. Meanwhile, Nate came in, looking sleepy.

When we were settled, Mr. Morgan thanked us for agreeing to meet so early.

"No problemo!" said Tessa. Then she took a sip and made a face. "Is this what coffee's supposed to taste like?"

Granny got her some sugar.

Mr. Morgan continued, "Mr. Webb and I started our investigation into the missing egg at the museum yesterday. But we've run into some roadblocks, and we're hoping you can help."

"Actually, Mr. Morgan," Tessa interrupted, "we have already solved the case."

Mr. Morgan looked surprised, but not half as surprised as me, Nate and Granny. "What are you talking about?" I asked.

Tessa waved her arms the way she does. "What Mom and Dad said last night—*duh!* President Manfred Alfredo-Chin stole the dinosaur egg!"

This was not the first time Tessa had changed her mind overnight. But Nate, Granny and Charlotte hadn't been there when Mom and Dad told us about the legend, so I filled them in.

"Thank you, Cameron," Mr. Morgan said. "Mr. Webb and I are also aware of the issues in a certain nearby nation. However, our initial investigation indicates they are irrelevant."

"What's 'ir-rel-e—'?" Tessa started to ask.

"Doesn't matter," Nate said.

"It matters to *me*!" Tessa said.

"I mean the word 'irrelevant' means it doesn't matter," Nate said. "So Mr. Morgan's saying President Alfredo-Chin didn't steal the dinosaur egg."

"That is our opinion at this time," said Mr. Morgan.

"Well, *that's* a relief," said Tessa. "But then who did?"

Sometimes I can't believe my sister. "Tessa—if they knew that, they wouldn't be asking us to help, would they?"

Tessa was ready to admit I was right—except before she could, Mr. Morgan proved I was wrong. "We are confident we know who stole the egg," he said. "Professor Cordell Bohn."

CHAPTER SEVEN

If I were dramatic like my sister, I would have jumped out of my chair, waved my arms and probably stomped my feet.

I liked Professor Bohn! He knew interesting stuff about dinosaurs, and besides, he was smiley and funny and not like the other so-serious grown-ups. I didn't want him to be an egg thief, and I didn't believe he was one, either.

But I am not dramatic like my sister. So what I did instead was ask very, very calmly, "How do you know?"

Mr. Morgan explained.

It turned out he and Mr. Webb had spent Saturday afternoon and evening interviewing Professor Bohn, Professor Rexington and a few other people. What they learned was that Professor Rexington had been waiting for the dinosaur egg to arrive from a certain nearby nation all week. Then, at lunchtime Friday, a wooden crate showed up on her desk.

"It was the right kind of crate with the right kind of

label," Mr. Morgan said. "Naturally, she assumed it was the dinosaur egg."

"Wait a second," said Tessa. "What do you mean it 'showed up'? Didn't someone bring it to her?"

"Someone must have, but she was at lunch, and we don't know who," Mr. Morgan said.

"Write that down, Cammie," Tessa said.

I held up my notebook so Tessa could see I already had. Tessa nodded. "Good work. So then what happened?"

Mr. Morgan explained that inside the crate, Professor Rexington found the gleaming, cream-colored ostrich egg, wrapped in crumpled newspaper and brown straw.

"She knew right away it belonged to an ostrich," said Mr. Morgan, "and she immediately notified Professor Bohn. Rather than being upset, he was amused. He told her he fully expected the egg fossil to show up later in the day."

"But it didn't," Nate said.

Mr. Morgan nodded. "And when it didn't, he decided to use the ostrich egg as a prop for his talk and see what happened. Meanwhile, they reported the missing egg to security."

"So that's where you come in," Nate said.

Mr. Morgan nodded. "We tried to trace the real dinosaur egg's route to the United States. Apparently, it was shipped from the airport in the capital of a certain nearby nation. The shipping records show the crate was scanned into the system when it arrived at Dulles airport here in the United States. After that, the crate seems to have disappeared. We think the thief must have picked it up from the airport here, but we can't find any record of that."

For a moment the room was quiet except for the sound of me writing. When I had caught up with my notes, I realized something: "This is all pretty mysterious, but none of it says Professor Bohn is the thief."

Mr. Webb said, "On the contrary," and I almost dropped my pen because that was five whole syllables, and Mr. Webb never says anything!

Mr. Morgan nodded. "We were suspicious. Why did Professor Bohn insist the ostrich egg was only a harmless prank?"

"Uh...," I said, "because that's what he really thought?"

"Or," said Mr. Morgan, "because he wanted to delay a full investigation as long as possible. And there is something else. Late last night we made a call to Washington's top ten p.m. news team: Jan and Larry."

"Hey, wow—what a coincidence," said Tessa. "We watch Jan and Larry, too!"

Mr. Morgan nodded. "Everybody does. And when Mr. Webb and I heard the broadcast last night, we zeroed in on one thing: the identity of the 'unnamed sources' who told them about the egg's link to politics in a certain nearby nation."

"Jan and Larry don't have to name their sources," Nate said. "Freedom of the press is protected by the First Amendment to the Constitution."

"True," said Mr. Morgan. "But when national security is involved, the news media is often willing to cooperate. Also, I went to high school with Jan."

"So who told them?" Tessa asked.

Mr. Morgan raised his eyebrows: "Professor Cordell Bohn."

Tessa shook her head. "Uh-oh, Cammie. This is not looking good."

Meanwhile, Granny said, "Let me see if I've got this straight. You think Professor Bohn called Jan and Larry to suggest that the theft was connected to politics. You think he was trying to shift attention away from the truth—that he's the thief."

Mr. Morgan nodded. "Exactly right."

I had more questions, but Charlotte looked at her watch. "Ahem? It is getting a bit late if the children are going to get to church."

Mr. Morgan and Mr. Webb stood up to leave. "We have a plane to catch." They were on their way to Pittsburgh, Professor Bohn's hometown, to continue their investigation.

"What do you want us to do?" Tessa asked.

"While we're confident we have identified the thief," said Mr. Morgan, "we lack the proof we need. What we're hoping you can do is help us get that proof."

CHAPTER EIGHT

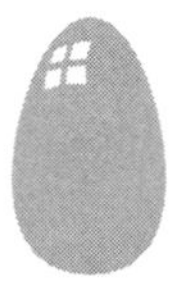

After fast good-byes, Granny hustled us into the Family Kitchen, which is also on the White House second floor. There, Tessa, Nate and I poured our coffee down the sink and grabbed bagels with peanut butter to eat on the way.

Downstairs, three cars were waiting for us. Granny goes to one church, Aunt Jen and Nate go to another—and my family goes to the Methodist one by Dupont Circle. It's the same one we started going to eight years ago when my mom got elected senator and we moved to Washington from California.

I like going to church. Mom, Dad, Tessa and I get to be together. We sing. The light coming through the stained-glass windows makes pretty patterns on the floor.

Because it was Palm Sunday, the service began with the choir coming in waving palm branches and calling, "Hosanna!" After that, we sang a hymn; then a lady read Bible verses about how Jesus was the prophet of Nazareth.

Finally, the pastor stood up to speak. I tried to pay attention, but I had so much to think about! Solving a new mystery and finding an ancient dinosaur egg sounded fun. Gathering evidence to prove a nice man was a thief? Not so fun. But maybe Mr. Morgan and Mr. Webb were wrong. Maybe the evidence would show that somebody else stole the dinosaur egg.

I remembered what Mr. Morgan had said about the case and realized right away there was something that didn't make sense, something that might be a clue: the wooden crate with the ostrich egg that showed up on Professor Rexington's desk.

How did it get there, anyway?

I pictured a crate floating through the entrance of the museum and pushing buttons on the elevator . . . and I cracked myself up, which made Mom, Dad and Tessa all look over at me.

Oops.

Sorry, I mouthed.

Now the minister was talking about Jesus riding on a donkey, which made me picture a crate on the back of a donkey . . . and soon I was thinking about the case again.

By the time the minister said he would see us all next week to celebrate Easter Sunday, I had thought up the first step of a plan to solve the mystery, find the dinosaur egg and—by the way—prove to Mr. Morgan and Mr. Webb that even if Professor Bohn liked to joke around, he wasn't actually a bad guy.

All I needed was a single, solitary secret weapon—which luckily was not a problem. Right now, the one I had in mind was probably having a late-morning snooze.

It didn't take much convincing to get Nate and Tessa to go along with my plan; neither of them had a better idea. So that same afternoon, the three of us—along with Malik, one of the Secret Service agents, and our secret weapon—were in a White House van on our way back to the National Museum of Natural History. It closes at five on Sunday, so by five-thirty it was pretty empty.

The secret weapon was on a leash, because otherwise I was pretty positive he'd chew up some ancient, priceless bone or spider or piece of an asteroid.

Like you've probably figured out, the weapon I'm talking about is Hooligan, our big furry mutt. Hooligan looks like a cross between an Afghan hound and a Dr. Seuss character, which my dad says is because he's a mad mix-up of just about every kind of dog ever. Last time we went detecting, we found out Hooligan's nose must've come from a bloodhound, because he sure can track a scent.

But was last time just beginner's luck?

We were about to find out.

CHAPTER NINE

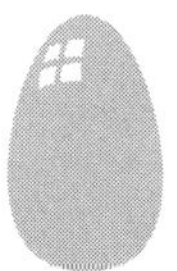

Professor Rexington met us inside the museum and led us through back hallways to a staff elevator that went up to the top floor, where her office is. Unlike Professor Bohn, Professor Rexington is not the most cheerful person ever. She hardly smiled when she said hello. But maybe she was just tired? There were circles under her eyes, same as my mom gets when she's stressed out.

Finally, we arrived at her office. The door was open, and we went in.

"You wanted to see the desk where the crate arrived, right? Well, this is it." Professor Rexington nodded at a big wooden desk with a neat stack of papers on top.

Meanwhile, our secret weapon wagged his tail and started sniffing inside a metal wastebasket beside the desk. It was full of crumpled newspaper and brown straw stuff.

"Oh, yeah," I said, "is that the packing material that was around the ostrich egg?"

Professor Rexington nodded. "Yes. I remember

thinking the straw looked like nesting material—appropriate for an egg."

"Can we see the crate, too?" Tessa asked.

Professor Rexington frowned. "I'm afraid I might've recycled it already–let me check."

She went through a door to another room and rustled around. While we waited, Hooligan continued to sniff.

"Good puppy! Smart puppy!" Tessa threw her arms around him. "You already know what you're supposed to do!"

My idea was for Hooligan to get the scent of the crate, then follow it backward from the desk. There are a ton of entrances to the museum. Knowing which one the crate came through might help us figure out how it got to the museum and who sent it.

Hooligan waited patiently for Tessa to be done hugging him; then he got back to work. At the same time, I knelt and looked at the date on the newspapers—Thursday, April 6, last Thursday. I pointed this out to Nate. He nodded and said since the crate arrived at the museum on Friday, it must have been packed and sent right away.

Meanwhile, Professor Rexington came back in with a slat of splintered wood and said, "Bad news. This is all that's left."

I examined the piece of wood, but there were no markings on it. Then I gave it to Hooligan to sniff. Did it smell like anything to him? Or were the different smells in the wastebasket confusing? For all I knew, somebody's lunch leftovers were in there.

My great idea didn't seem so great anymore. But it was too late to worry about that now. I would just have to trust our dog.

"Ready?" I said.

Malik, Tessa and Nate nodded.

"Okay." I took the leash and stood up. "Hooligan—go find!"

CHAPTER TEN

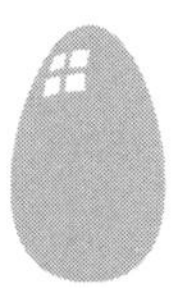

Note to self: next time you track anything with Hooligan, let Malik hold the leash.

Hooligan was so excited and took off so fast he nearly separated my arm from my shoulder, not to mention that no one could keep up with us.

"Hoo-Hoo-Hooligan! Slow down!" Tessa whined, but our dog didn't listen. Instead, nose held high, he galloped one way then the other down the corridors.

Was he really tracking a scent?

Or did he think we were playing tag?

Whatever it was, he was having a great time, and only skidded to a stop when he reached an impenetrable barrier—closed elevator doors.

This was a different elevator from the one we came up in. Nate, Tessa, Malik and Professor Rexington were way behind us by now, and before they could come near, Hooligan did one of the amazing tricks he's learned since coming to live in the White House: he jumped up and pushed the elevator call button with his paw.

The elevator car must've been waiting, because the doors opened instantly, and Hooligan looked around like, *We don't have to wait for those slowpokes, do we, Cammie?*

Well, of course we had to wait for them! I am not allowed to go anywhere without the Secret Service, in this case Malik—and he was bringing up the rear so he could keep Tessa and Nate in sight.

Thinking, *No problem, I know how to hold an elevator,* I let Hooligan tug me inside, but then, before I could stop him, he did it again—jumped up and pushed a button on the panel.

"Oh, no you don't!" I started looking frantically for the button that opens the doors, but there were a lot of floors in the building and a lot of buttons, too! By the time I finally found the right one, the doors were shut and the elevator had creaked into gear.

"Hooligan!" I said. *"Bad dog!"*

He didn't pay any attention, just sniffed the air, the walls and the corners. He was tracking something, but was it an ancient dinosaur egg? Or a stale turkey sandwich?

Down, down and down the elevator dropped into the museum's unknown depths. On the way, I had plenty of time to think . . . and to worry. When finally we came to rest, we were someplace called Level D.

D for Dungeon?

The second the doors cracked open, Hooligan shot

through, dragging me so fast my shoulders bumped one after the other—*Ouch! ouch!*—and before I even blinked, we were galloping top speed down what I think was a corridor, but I'm not sure because it was pitch-black and I couldn't see a thing!

CHAPTER ELEVEN

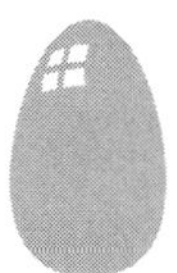

Can dogs see in the dark the way cats can? Why, oh, why, had I never looked this up?

I don't know how long we ran or where we went, but just when my legs were ready to quit, Hooligan put on a burst of speed, the leash slipped out of my hand and I flew headlong into something big and solid and . . . *furry*?

Still blind, I backed up and hit another hard, furry something, turned left and . . . *Ouch!*—something sharp! A claw? A tooth?—then right and . . . *bump, tumble, somersault*—I was suddenly sitting on the cold, hard floor and trapped for sure, with big, furry, sharp-clawed somethings closing in around me.

What did I do?

I screamed!

And then the lights came on. Now it was glare that blinded me, but I could still hear—the *click-click-clickety* of galloping doggy toenails, and then a man's voice: "What is going on in here?"

I blinked; my eyes focused, and here came my faithful dog on a mission to rescue me not only from this grumpy man but from a room full of life-size lions and tigers and bears—oh, my!

They were everywhere, each one stiff and staring just like the big African elephant in the rotunda upstairs.

Hooligan plowed into me a second later—*Oof!*—and licked my face—*Ewww!*—and for a few moments I just sat there breathing while the grumpy man sputtered about "unauthorized kids" and "trespassing" and "valuable exhibits."

Then he got a good look at me. "Y-y-you're Cameron Parks!"

I nodded. "Yes, I am. And I'm very sorry to be trespassing. And if you'll give me a second, I'll explain."

By the time Malik, Nate, Tessa and Professor Rexington arrived, Mr. Clark had introduced himself, and I had told him how Hooligan was tracking a wooden crate that used to contain an ostrich egg. Level D was not the dungeon. It was a subbasement storage area for old museum exhibits like these stuffed hunting trophies.

Hooligan wasn't done tracking yet, and now, trotting at a reasonable speed, he led us out of the storage room and down a corridor to a battered old desk by a set of double garage-type doors. Mr. Clark explained that the desk was his and that this part of the building was a loading dock.

Meanwhile, Hooligan sat himself down and looked up expectantly. As far as he was concerned, this was the finish line, he had won the race and now he wanted his prize.

I said, "Good puppy!" and pulled a doggy treat from my pocket and gave it to him.

Mr. Clark said, "There's a driveway and a ramp outside for delivery trucks, but it's not as big as the new one, so it's not used much anymore. Sometimes I think everybody upstairs"—he looked at Professor Rexington—"has forgotten us."

Tessa folded her arms across her chest like she always does when she's interviewing a witness. "Mr. Clark, do you keep track of what's delivered here?"

Mr. Clark looked offended. "That's my job." He pulled a fat black binder out of his desk. "What day are you interested in?"

Tessa said Friday morning, and Mr. Clark turned a couple of pages. "Is it this one?" he asked. "One of my coworkers entered it. I don't work Friday mornings."

The entry read: "Received 11:55 a.m., from Red Heart Delivery, one wooden crate weighing 15 pounds, 4 ounces. Destination 8th floor, office of Professor Rexington."

"Jackpot, Cammie!" Tessa said.

"Yeah, whaddya know?" Nate said. "Your plan actually worked."

"It's Hooligan who should get the credit," I said modestly. But actually I was pretty proud. Now all we had to do was phone Red Heart Delivery, find out who had sent the crate and bingo—we had cracked the case of the missing dinosaur egg!

CHAPTER TWELVE

We thanked Mr. Clark and Professor Rexington and said good-bye. Then Malik drove us back to the White House. On the way, I slipped our secret weapon one more doggy treat. He deserved it.

At home, we wanted to look up Red Heart Delivery right away and call, but we were already late for dinner. Mom, Dad and Aunt Jen were busy, so we kids were supposed to eat with Granny in the Family Kitchen—and she likes to eat at six-thirty sharp.

We had tuna casserole with noodles and peas, which maybe doesn't sound that delicious, but there were fried bread crumbs on top, and homemade applesauce, too. When Granny gets sick of being waited on by the White House staff, she likes to cook for us.

While we ate, we took turns telling her what had happened at the museum. When we were done, she said, "I just have one question. You found the crumpled newspaper the egg was packed in—"

"It was dated Thursday, April sixth," said Nate. "We made sure to check."

Granny nodded. "Good... and what newspaper was it?"

Tessa, Nate and I looked at each other. None of us had noticed—and we should have—*duh.* The town the newspaper came from might tell us the town the ostrich egg came from!

Granny saw we felt dumb, so she tried an easier question. "Was the newspaper written in English?"

I thought for a second. "Yes, because I could read the date."

Granny nodded. "In that case, it didn't come from a certain nearby nation. They don't speak English there."

"So President Manfred Alfredo-Chin couldn't have packed the ostrich egg," I said. "He must not be the thief... unless he has helpers in an English-speaking place."

"We already know Professor Bohn is the thief, Cammie," Tessa said. "And when we call Red Heart Delivery, we're going to find out that Professor Bohn's the one who sent the egg."

I didn't think so.

And I was right.

But for all the wrong reasons.

After we put the dishes in the dishwasher, we went up to Nate's room on the third floor to use his computer. He looked all over the Web, but he couldn't find Red Heart Delivery anywhere.

So we trooped back downstairs to find Granny, who was reading in the West Sitting Hall, and she got up and looked till she found an old paper phone book in a drawer in the Family Kitchen.

There was no Red Heart Delivery there, either.

“Maybe they don’t want publicity,” Tessa said.

“All businesses want publicity,” Granny said. “Otherwise, how do they get customers?”

“Then why can’t we find them?” Nate asked.

“Only one reason I can think of,” said Granny. “Because they don’t exist.”

“Well, *that’s* disappointing!” Tessa said.

“A dead end.” I sighed. “What do we do now?”

Granny shrugged. “When you come to a dead end, you try another direction.”

And the next day, Monday, that’s just what I did.

CHAPTER THIRTEEN

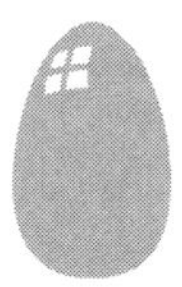

I'm in fifth grade, and Monday is the day fifth graders have library after lunch.

For our investigation, this turned out to be lucky, because Mr. Brackbill, the school librarian, likes to give us Internet research assignments.

That day the assignment was: Find five dinosaur facts from five reliable websites.

Dinosaur facts—*yes!*

Even better, we were allowed to pick our own partners, and right away I looked around for Evgenia. She is one of those quiet kinds of people you don't notice till one day she says something that is seriously smart.

"I have an idea for what to research," I said as soon as we sat down at the computer table. "Not that long ago, a dinosaur egg fossil was found in a certain nearby nation. Let's look that up. I mean"—I suddenly realized that might sound bossy—"unless you have a better idea."

Evgenia grinned as she logged us in to the computer. "You're detecting again, aren't you? When Jan and Larry talked about that missing egg last week? I thought, 'That sounds exactly like a job for the First Kids!'"

We started by searching "dinosaur egg" and the name of the certain nearby nation. Bingo—we got lots of results from science magazines, newspapers, museums and TV stations. One of them included both Professor Rexington and Professor Bohn, so we tried that one first, and . . . guess what?

We found out the two paleontologists don't like each other at all!

It's not because of personal stuff. It's because of science. I didn't understand everything in the article, but basically they disagree about whether the dinosaur that laid the missing egg is a close relative of birds that live today. Professor Bohn thinks it is, and Professor Rexington thinks it's not.

I guess if you're a scientist, you think this kind of stuff is worth fighting about.

Anyway, the reason the dinosaur egg was coming to the United States at all was so Professor Rexington and Professor Bohn could study the shell. Each one thought its structure would prove he—or she—was right.

Evgenia and I looked at some more websites and found a picture of the missing dinosaur egg. I couldn't help thinking the scientists who found it had to have been pretty smart even to have recognized that a gray, oval-shaped rock was really an egg fossil.

Mr. Brackbill would give us extra credit for having

a picture, so I copied and pasted it into my document. Then I typed these facts:

- The egg was found last fall by Professor Rexington, Professor Bohn and a team of scientists from the nearby nation.
- It probably came from a dinosaur called Unenlagia that was probably about six feet tall and had feathers.
- The Unenlagia dinosaur could flap its front legs the way birds flap their wings.
- "Unenlagia" means "half-bird" in a South American language.

We still needed another fact, and Evgenia saw that there was an article about the egg on the website of a certain nearby nation. Luckily, it was written in English, but what it said was totally different from the other ones:

The American scientists who found this so-called dinosaur egg are mistaken. Their ignorance can be seen very easily by the fact that they recently mistook an ostrich egg for a dinosaur egg at a presentation at an important museum in the capital of the United States of America.

In fact, the so-called dinosaur egg discovered in our nation last year belonged to a large bird that has been extinct for one century only. As every schoolchild in our nation knows, no animal or plant life lived within our borders until long after the time of the dinosaurs.

Evgenia's eyes got big. "This is totally the opposite of everything else we've been reading!"

"And it isn't very nice about Professor Bohn and Professor Rexington, either," I said.

"Mr. Brackbill says just because you find something on the Internet doesn't make it true," Evgenia said. "You have to cross-check and consider sources."

"I guess he's right," I said. "Let's look up when the Unenlagia dinosaur lived."

Evgenia went back to the Smithsonian website and found the answer. Then she added:

- Unenlagia lived in the Mesozoic period, about 90 million years ago.

I couldn't wait to tell Nate and Tessa what I had learned, so of course the rest of the school day passed extra slowly. Finally, at 3:15, I was set free. Jeremy was driving the van that met us out front. Granny was in back.

I started explaining about the library before I was even buckled in. When I was finished, Nate said, "Good job, Cameron! Now we know why Professor Bohn stole the egg. He wanted to keep it away from Professor Rexington."

Uh-oh. I never thought of that! I started to argue, but Granny interrupted with news of her own.

"Since you children were busy in school, I did a little

detecting myself." Granny knows all about detecting. She used to be a police officer. "That newspaper in Professor Rexington's wastebasket? It was the *Washington Post.* So it seems whoever sent the ostrich egg must have packed it up right here in town."

Tessa grinned. "Good job, Granny! Mr. Morgan and Mr. Webb will be super proud. They've only been gone since yesterday, and already we've gathered two pieces of evidence to help prove it was Professor Bohn who stole the dinosaur egg."

CHAPTER FOURTEEN

What was I doing wrong?

Solving the case was supposed to prove Professor Bohn was innocent. But so far it seemed more like the opposite.

I needed to think. So after Tessa, Nate and I had eaten our snack, I asked Granny if she thought Mr. Bryant would let me take Hooligan for a walk around the South Lawn.

Mr. Bryant used to operate the Presidential Elevator, but now he works for our family, taking care of Hooligan on weekdays.

"I'm sure Mr. Bryant will be happy for the coffee break," Granny said. "But Charlotte will have to go with you."

"I know," I said.

"And we'll have to alert the other officers outside."

"I know."

"And mind the public, Cameron. Don't talk to anybody—and remember, they're all voters or potential voters."

When Granny said "the public," she meant the people outside the White House fence looking in. I'm not supposed to actually talk to these people, because I might say something dumb by mistake that would get on the news and be embarrassing. On the other hand, I should always smile and be polite, because if I don't, people might not vote for Mom.

"I know, Granny. I am a representative of the family."

Granny smiled, then reached over and gave my shoulder a squeeze. "Living in the White House is a bother sometimes, Cameron. But there are a lot of privileges, too. You're looking forward to the Easter egg roll, aren't you?"

An Easter egg roll is a race where you push a hard-boiled egg with a spoon. The tradition started at the White House way back in the 1800s, and now thousands of people come to the South Lawn the day after Easter to celebrate. There are games and music and food—kind of like a church picnic, only bigger.

I nodded. "I'm looking forward to the fried rice, too," I said, which made Granny laugh. The first time Tessa ever heard of an Easter egg roll, she thought it was Chinese food.

While Granny got hold of Charlotte and Mr. Bryant, I went to Tessa's and my bedroom to put on jeans and sneakers. Then I read over my notes for the case so they'd be fresh in my mind.

On my way downstairs, I stopped by Hooligan's room. Tessa was there, sitting on the floor by the kittens—two orange, one black, and three gray tabbies—a squirming mass of fur and cuteness. I reached in and tickled the mama, who flicked her tail but didn't bother to wake up.

"The kitten book says they'll be more fun next week when they can see and hear," Tessa said. "But they'll be messier, too. Right now the mama cleans up most of the disgusting parts."

I said, "No wonder she's tired." Then I told Tessa I was going out to walk Hooligan and think.

"About the case?" she asked.

I nodded.

"You don't think Professor Bohn stole the egg, do you?"

"It's obvious, huh?"

"*Hello-o-o?* I'm your *sister*! But we don't get to pick who did it, Cammie. Like Granny says, we have to be fair and look at the evidence."

"I'm trying," I said. "But the truth is, I'd rather it was somebody else—like Professor Rexington. She's not nearly as nice. And she has a motive, too, right? She wants the egg as much as Professor Bohn does. She wants to prove she's the one who's right about birds and dinosaurs."

Tessa said, "I wasn't going to tell you this, but I thought of something else. Why did Professor Rexington recycle the crate so fast?"

I shrugged. "Because she's super well organized? You saw how tidy her office was."

"Maybe," said Tessa, "or maybe because the crate had a return address or some other clue. Maybe there was something she didn't want us to see."

I stared at my sister. "I should've thought of that!"

Tessa said, "Why? Because you're older?"

"No, because I'm smarter—*duh.*" And then I had to move fast because Tessa was scrambling to her feet, ready to pound me.

CHAPTER FIFTEEN

I got away from my sister okay.

All I had to do was call over my shoulder, "I take it back! You're smart, too!" then run down two flights of stairs and cross into the Diplomatic Reception Room, which is how you get to the South Lawn.

Mr. Bryant and Charlotte met me under the awning outside, and Mr. Bryant handed me Hooligan's leash.

"I appreciate your taking over for a few minutes, Cameron. Your grandmother is putting on a pot of coffee." Then he gave Hooligan a pat on the head. "You behave yourself. Understand?"

Hooligan answered by sitting politely and displaying his most noble profile.

Charlotte rolled her eyes. "Sometimes I think this dog should travel with his personal photographer."

"Yeah," I said, "he has a lot in common with my sister that way."

"Where shall we walk?" Charlotte asked after Mr. Bryant left to go meet Granny.

I said, "Children's Garden," which is a part of the South Lawn that has a path and a pond and a climbing tree. A First Lady a long time ago had it built for when her grandchildren came to visit.

Charlotte and I turned right toward the West Wing, where my mom's office is. Nearing it, I saw her and a cluster of other people walking in the Rose Garden. Right away, I noticed one of the men because he wasn't wearing a suit like everybody else. Instead, he had on an untucked, short-sleeve white shirt and black pants....

Wait a sec. Hadn't there been a guy at Professor Bohn's museum talk in a shirt like that?

I pointed him out to Charlotte, who told me that kind of shirt is called a guayabera—pronounced "gwy-uh-bear-uh"—and they're popular in countries where it's hot.

"Who are those guys, anyway?" I asked her.

Charlotte squinted at them. "I'm not sure. Foreign dignitaries, I guess."

A foreign dignitary is somebody important who comes from another country. Before I could ask where these ones were from, I got distracted by Hooligan, who had stopped to sniff the air.

Uh-oh.

This could be trouble.

I got a good grip on his leash...but not good enough, because half a second later he bolted for the Rose Garden, tugging me off-balance and yanking the leash out of my hand.

"Hooligan!" I tried to call, but only the first syl-

lable came out. The second two were muted by the combination of grass and earth my face encountered on the ground—*owieee!*

"Cammie, are you okay?" Charlotte reached down to help me. I wiped the dirt out of my eyes and saw Hooligan was on a collision course with Mom and the foreign dignitaries.

Charlotte cringed. "I hope they're from a friendly country."

Me, too, because by now, Hooligan had zeroed in on his intended target—none other than the man in the guayabera shirt—and was gathering himself to make a leap.

The man must not have been expecting a big, furry, flying impact, because—*pow!*—when Hooligan connected—*ouch!*—he toppled over backward.

"Oh, dear," I said, "I hope that guy likes dogs."

CHAPTER SIXTEEN

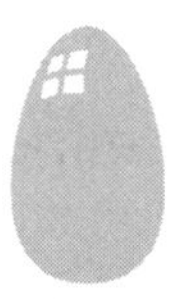

The guy did not like dogs.

Especially big dogs that jump on you, knock you over and slobber on your face.

But it's not like he had to go to the hospital or anything.

And Mom said the White House laundry might be able to wash the paw prints out if he didn't mind handing over his shirt.

There are always newspeople at the White House, and now—as the guy was helped to his feet—their cameras whirred and clicked.

Meanwhile, my mom introduced us. "This is my daughter Cameron, Mr. Valenteen. And she is about to apologize for our dog's terrible behavior."

"I'm really sorry," I said. "I don't know why Hooligan did that. Usually he only attacks squirrels and pigeons."

"I am not a squirrel or a pigeon," Mr. Valenteen said.

"I can see that," I said.

"Good. Then we're all in agreement," said Mom.

"Cameron, I'll see you at dinner. Gentlemen? Shall we continue our discussions inside?"

Mom, Mr. Valenteen and the guys in suits turned and headed for my mom's office. Meanwhile, Hooligan sat himself down in good-dog fashion and looked up at me expectantly.

"What's with you, anyway?" I asked him. "You don't get a doggy treat for jumping on some poor, random guy. You know that, right?"

But apparently he didn't know that, because he cocked his head and woofed a sad and disappointed little *woof.*

"Was he the same man from the museum?" Charlotte asked me. "Or just wearing the same kind of shirt?"

"Same man," I said. "Weird, huh? I guess he must be interested in dinosaurs."

We turned toward the Children's Garden, and I asked Charlotte if she'd mind helping me go over the evidence.

"Happy to," she said. "After all, I am a law enforcement professional. What do you know so far?"

Since I had just reviewed my notes, it was easy to tell her the important parts:

- Jan and Larry said the dinosaur egg might be missing because of politics in a certain nearby nation.
- Professor Bohn was the "unnamed source" who told them that.

- The crate had been scanned in at Dulles airport on Thursday.
- The packing newspaper was the *Washington Post*, dated last Thursday.
- The delivery company, Red Heart, didn't exist.
- Professor Rexington and Professor Bohn were in a feud about the family history of dinosaurs and birds.

By this time we had passed the tennis courts and gone under the trellis into the garden, which is surrounded by trees and bushes. A path leads to the goldfish pond, and children and grandchildren of past presidents have left their handprints in the concrete paving stones. I hopscotched over the names "Jenna Bush" and "Barbara Bush," then sat down in one of the white metal chairs by the pond.

Instead of checking out the goldfish, Hooligan lay down next to me and closed his eyes. It must be hard work, attacking foreign dignitaries.

"Mr. Morgan and Mr. Webb say Professor Bohn is the thief, but I'm not sure," I told Charlotte. "Maybe instead, the egg's disappearance is connected to a certain nearby nation."

"That's where Mr. Valenteen is from," Charlotte said. "I only realized it when I saw the dignitaries close-up. With all the prodemocracy protests there, they want your mom to reaffirm the U.S.'s alliance with President Manfred Alfredo-Chin."

"What does that mean—reaffirm the alliance?" I asked.

"Tell all the other countries the United States still likes him," Charlotte said.

I thought for a second. "So it's the same as when my best friend, Courtney Lozana, ate the last cookie out of my lunch? And I got mad, but the next day she gave me a bag of chips and told me to tell all our other friends how I wasn't mad at her anymore so they wouldn't be mad at her, either?"

Charlotte looked thoughtful. "Pretty much, yeah. Sometimes countries act a lot like fifth graders. But none of that is helping you with your case. I have a question. Maybe you said, but I missed it. Where did that ostrich egg come from?"

For a second, I felt annoyed. Usually I like Charlotte, because even though I'm a kid, she listens to me. But now it was like she hadn't heard me at all. "From the crate at the museum and before that from Red Heart Delivery," I repeated.

"Yeah, yeah, I got all that," Charlotte said. "But *before* that. The egg was ready to hatch, so it probably came from nearby. There can't be that many places to get an ostrich egg around here. So maybe if you found the place where the egg was laid?"

I sat still for a moment, listening to the pond burble and watching a tan cardinal and her red boyfriend doing a jig by its edge. Then I said, "Charlotte, you're a genius."

CHAPTER SEVENTEEN

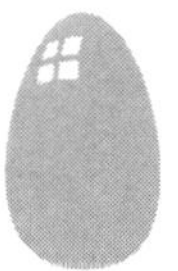

Charlotte was not only a genius. She was right. There aren't many places around Washington to get an ostrich egg. In fact, there is only one: Mega Bird Farm, located in the country about thirty miles from the White House.

That was the result that came back when Nate went online and entered "ostrich farm Washington D.C." into the search engine right before dinner.

"I'll call them!" Tessa volunteered. She always likes to do the talking.

"You can give it a try," I said. "Ask them if—"

"I *know* what to ask, Cammie." Tessa had already picked up the phone on Nate's desk and was dialing the number on the website. After a few seconds, she said, "Hello? This is Tessa Parks, and . . . yes, that Tessa Parks, and . . . yes, I am totally serious."

I didn't have to hear the other side of the conversation to imagine it. A lot of times when one of us calls somebody we don't know, they don't believe we're really us.

"Thank you," Tessa went on. "I think she's a good president, too. Anyway, my sister and my cousin and I are investigating a case, and we have some questions for you.... Uh, hold on a sec, would you?" Tessa looked up at me and Nate. "What are our questions, again?"

"Ask if somebody bought an egg last week," Nate said.

"And if somebody did buy an egg, who was it?" I said.

Tessa repeated the questions, listened and nodded. "Oh, really? Okay, I'll check.... And you have a very mega day, too!" She hung up.

"Well?" Nate and I said at the same time.

"She doesn't like to give information out over the phone," Tessa said. "But I should still have a very mega day."

"So we have to go out there?" I said.

Tessa grinned and pumped her fist. *"Road trip!"*

A road trip sounded good to me, too. The problem was that when you're the president's kid, a road trip is not so easy. The Secret Service would have to go with us and they would have to scout the place in advance. Since they have other things to do, arrangements might take a while. The question was, how long?

At dinner, we told Granny we wanted to visit Mega Bird Farm, and she agreed it was a good idea. After dinner, she called to talk to the Secret Service about how soon we could go. Tessa, Nate and I were finishing our homework in the solarium when Charlotte came in to deliver the bad news.

"Friday after school?" Tessa waved her arms the way she does. "But what will we tell Mr. Morgan and Mr. Webb? They are going to be *so-o-o* disappointed!"

"I thought of that," Charlotte said, "so I got in touch with them already. They're having such a good time in Pittsburgh, they've decided to stay a few more days. But they said don't worry, and they promise to call when they get back."

CHAPTER EIGHTEEN

A lot of times I am surprised by the stuff the news guys think is important. For example, remember when Hooligan knocked over that foreign dignitary—Mr. Valenteen?

That was on Monday afternoon, and for the rest of the week, it was like you couldn't turn on the TV or look at the Web without seeing Hooligan leaping, the guy's face looking scared and unhappy, and then Hooligan again—showing off his profile like he was proud he had knocked somebody over.

As you can imagine, this was all pretty embarrassing for my mom and the rest of the United States government.

So on Thursday when Tessa's and my friend Toni called to invite us and Nate and Hooligan over to her house, my mom was happy. In case you don't remember, Toni's father is the ambassador from Mr. Valenteen's nation. According to Mom, the invitation was supposed to be a sign that the people there were ready to forgive Hooligan and the American people.

Tessa disagreed. "I don't think the invitation is a sign of anything," she said. "I think Toni just invited us because we're friends. Plus Toni told me there's this cool new rock in her rock collection and she wants us to see it."

The invitation was for Easter after lunch. Toni's family lives in the ambassador's house, which is next to the office part of the embassy in the neighborhood of Washington, D.C. called Georgetown. Hooligan was included because he's friends with Toni's dog, Ozzabelle. While we checked out the rocks, they were going to have a playdate.

Besides the invitation from Toni, a few other things happened that week:

- I studied my spelling words for the Friday test and did math homework.
- Tessa and I tried on our Easter dresses to make sure they fit.
- The kittens opened their eyes the rest of the way.
- Tessa, Nate, the Easter Bunny and I assembled baskets to be given as prizes at the Easter egg roll. (The Easter Bunny was really one of my mom's staffers dressed up in a costume he told us was hot and itchy.)
- We got a postcard from Mr. Morgan and Mr. Webb. It showed a picture of a big, swoopy bridge over

the Ohio River, and it said: "Happy Detecting! See you next week!"

Finally it was Friday, and after school Granny and Charlotte picked us up in one of the White House vans.

Malik drove, and we went northwest out of the city into Maryland. For the first part, the scenery was mostly office buildings, but after a while we were in the country—big houses and rolling green hills with pink-flowering trees and red-flowering bushes.

Tessa fell asleep.

Nate asked, "Are we there yet?"

After we left the highway we drove on back roads for a while till we rounded a bend and saw a sign that read MEGA BIRD FARM.

I elbowed Tessa, who opened her eyes, looked out the window and squealed: "Are those for real?"

CHAPTER NINETEEN

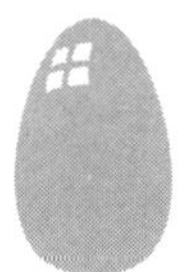

Yes, Tessa, they were for real—a flock of about fifty ostriches jogging alongside the van as it wound its way up a steep and curving driveway. I was glad the ostriches were on the other side of a chain-link fence.

Charlotte said they looked like long-legged feather dusters, and Nate said they looked like they had snakes for necks.

I thought they for sure looked a lot more like dinosaurs than they did like Granny's canary, or a cardinal, or any other normal bird.

At the end of the driveway was a one-story blue building with a covered porch and a sign on the door that said OPEN. Malik pulled into a parking space in front, and we all climbed out. An SUV was there already. It didn't have writing on it or anything, but I knew it belonged to the Secret Service. Some agents would have come out ahead of us just to make sure things were okay. Now they were hanging around nearby but out of sight.

The door of the blue building opened, and a smiling woman with frizzy gray hair came out. "Welcome! I'm Nancy Aviano, and most of you I recognize from the TV. It's Tessa I spoke to on the phone, correct?"

"Correct-amento!" said Tessa. She introduced Granny, Charlotte, Malik and me, and we all shook hands.

"I know you have some questions," Nancy Aviano said, "but first can I show you around?"

"Yes, please!" said Tessa. "I have never in my life met a grown-up ostrich before."

Mrs. Aviano turned out to be the same amount chatty as she was nice. Luckily, ostriches are interesting, so we didn't mind listening . . . and listening.

First she led us over to the fence so we could look at the ostriches and they could look back at us. From my bird book, I already knew a lot of what Mrs. Aviano was saying—how ostriches are native to Africa, run forty-five miles per hour and live as long as fifty years.

But reading a book isn't the same as seeing something close-up. Ostriches are awesome! They have huge eyes and long eyelashes, so their faces look friendly even if the rest of them looks weird. They're bigger than NBA players, up to nine feet tall and 350 pounds. They're super curious. One tried to peck Granny's bracelet, and another went for Charlotte's watch.

"They won't hurt you," Mrs. Aviano said, "unless you scare them. If they feel threatened, they kick, and I'm here to tell you that big toenail packs a wallop."

Next Mrs. Aviano showed us the barn where the ostriches are fed, and the shed she uses as a nursery.

Inside, there were heated boxes called incubators for the eggs, and bigger boxes called brooders for the young chicks. The older chicks had a separate room. They were clumsy and funny and covered with downy, spotted feathers that looked more like fur.

"Awww," Tessa said. "I wish we could've kept Dino. I bet Hooligan would've loved him."

"Hooligan probably would have tried to beat up on Dino when he was a chick," Nate said. "Then what a surprise when Dino grew up and wanted revenge!"

Mrs. Aviano asked who Dino was, and how was Hooligan, anyway? Like everyone else in America, she had seen our dog on TV plenty of times. As we walked back to the office, we explained how Hooligan really is good—he just has too much energy.

Then Tessa said, "And Dino is the reason we're here. Cammie, do you have your notebook?"

I held it up. "I'm ready."

Inside, Mrs. Aviano settled into her desk chair, and Tessa crossed her arms over her chest like she always does when she's going to ask questions.

Only, the way it turned out, she didn't even have to.

CHAPTER TWENTY

"You know," Mrs. Aviano began before Tessa had said a word, "you're not the only ones who want to know about that egg. A black-haired lady came out earlier in the week with the same question, and I told her what I'm going to tell you, namely that I never got the fellow's name because he paid cash.

"He showed up last Thursday without phoning ahead. He wanted an egg that had already been incubated, he said. It was an unusual request, but he assured me he'd be able to take care of the chick."

Tessa said, "Do you remember—"

"What he looked like? Average height. Average face. Average age. Now, if he'd been an ostrich, then I'd've paid more attention to details."

Tessa tried again. "What about—"

"The black-haired lady?" Mrs. Aviano shrugged. "She was out here the day before yesterday—Wednesday—and I would call her average-looking. Oh—but she had an accent. A foreign accent. And she told me her name—"

"Yes?" said Tessa.

"—but I forgot it."

By now, our visit to Mega Bird Farm was reminding me of our visit to the museum with Hooligan—interesting but a detecting dead end.

And Tessa was frustrated enough that she actually asked for help. "Can you guys think of anything?" She looked at me and Nate.

I shrugged, but Nate said, "Mrs. Aviano, you don't happen to have security cameras, do you? Video cameras?"

"Are you kidding?" said Mrs. Aviano. "A breeding pair of ostriches is worth a hundred thousand dollars! Of course we've got security cameras! You wanna see video of those visitors? Heck—why didn't you say so?"

The video playback was on the computer, so Tessa, Nate and I gathered around Mrs. Aviano's desk to watch. Setting everything up, Mrs. Aviano explained that the cameras only turn on when something moves near them. Because of that, there isn't that much video, and it only took about two seconds to find what we wanted.

The video shot Wednesday morning showed a lady with black hair standing at the counter in the office. When Mrs. Aviano paused the video, Tessa said, "Zoom in so we can see her face."

"Please," I added.

Mrs. Aviano tapped a key, and the lady's face filled

the screen. It was a little blurry, but you could tell she was probably older than my mom or Aunt Jen, and she had pale skin, a straight nose and small eyes. Her black hair was short. She was frowning.

None of us had ever seen her before, and neither—when we called her over to look—had Charlotte.

Next Mrs. Aviano pulled up the video from the day the average-looking man bought the egg. There was footage of him at the counter in the office, too, but the best picture was one in the incubator room. When Mrs. Aviano zoomed in, we all gasped, and Mrs. Aviano said, "Now that I look at him again, he does seem kind of familiar."

"Yeah, he does," said Tessa. "He's been on TV approximately one zillion times since Hooligan knocked him over in the Rose Garden on Monday. His name is Mr. Valenteen, and he's a foreign dignitary from a certain nearby nation."

CHAPTER TWENTY-ONE

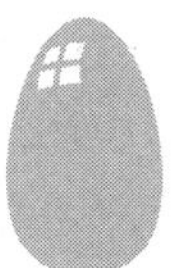

In the van on the way back to the White House, Tessa waved her arms and announced: "The case is solved. Mr. Valenteen did it!"

Granny said, *"Hmmm,"* and the way she said *"Hmmm,"* you could tell it meant "or not."

Tessa scowled. "What?"

"You're right that Mr. Valenteen must have delivered the ostrich egg to the museum," Granny said. "In fact, I think you may also have solved the mystery of why Hooligan knocked him over in the Rose Garden. Either the egg smelled like Mr. Valenteen—or Mr. Valenteen smelled like the egg."

"Oh, so that's why Hooligan expected a reward!" I said.

"And I thought of something, too," said Nate. "The name of the delivery company was Red Heart, right? Like Valentine's Day?"

Tessa smacked her forehead. *"Duh!* So Mr. *Valenteen*'s the one who invented the delivery company that doesn't exist!"

Granny nodded. "You've done a solid job on the ostrich egg. But you still don't know what happened to the egg that matters, the dinosaur egg."

Shoot. As usual, Granny was right.

"We know Professor Rexington and Professor Bohn found it in a certain nearby nation," I said. "And we know their colleagues there shipped it to the United States. Then, according to Mr. Morgan and Mr. Webb, it arrived at the airport here. . . . And after that, it disappeared."

"Right," said Granny. "So where is it?"

Tessa, Nate and I looked at each other. We had no idea.

"Besides that," Granny said, "as far as we know, Mr. Morgan and Mr. Webb are still convinced the real thief is Professor Bohn."

"Maybe there's a connection we don't know about between Professor Bohn and Mr. Valenteen," Nate said.

"And what about the lady with black hair?" Granny asked. "How is she connected?"

"She must not know Mr. Valenteen, anyway," I said. "Because if she did, she would've known he bought the ostrich egg, and she wouldn't have gone to Mega Bird Farm to ask."

Granny said, "I have another thought. There are two sides to the political troubles in a certain nearby nation—the prodemocracy side that wants new elections, and President Alfredo-Chin's side that doesn't. What if the lady and Mr. Valenteen are on opposite sides?"

"Which side is Mr. Valenteen on?" Tessa asked.

"President Manfred Alfredo-Chin's—*duh*," said

Nate, "because he works for President Chin's embassy here in Washington."

Malik piped up from the driver's seat: "I know someone on the prodemocracy side."

Charlotte was riding shotgun. "Who's that?"

Instead of answering, Malik pressed some buttons on the dashboard music player, and a song came on. It had a good beat but lame, lovey-dovey lyrics. Nate stuck a finger down his throat, but then—to my horror—Granny started singing along:

Lina is gone,
The woman is gone.
Left a note on my door,
Couldn't take any more. . . .

We kids all looked at each other. This had to stop. Granny was totally embarrassing herself in front of Charlotte and Malik!

I opened my mouth to say something—but before I could, Charlotte and Malik solved the problem. They started singing, too!

Lina is gone,
The woman is gone.
A fool always fails
And ends in love's jail. . . .

I tried hard to pretend I was somewhere else. Then I

realized I recognized the song. It was one my dad used to play when I was little.

"Hey—isn't that Eb Ghanamamma?" I said.

Malik grinned at me in the rearview mirror, then—still singing—nudged Charlotte and nodded at the glove compartment. Charlotte opened it and pulled out an old, beat-up CD case, which she handed back to Tessa and me.

The title was *Lina and Other Loves*, and on the front was a picture of Eb Ghanamamma himself—curly black hair, dark eyes, a crooked nose and a skinny face. His expression was what Mom would call "pouty."

Eb Ghanamamma, in case you don't know, is a famous folk singer from a certain nearby nation. Like Malik said, he is also one of the protesters against the government of President Manfred Alfredo-Chin. I know that because—even though we have never actually met—Eb Ghanamamma helped Tessa, Nate and me solve the Case of the Diamond Dog Collar.

Malik was turning the van into the White House's East Gate when Granny looked over her shoulder at us and said, "So by now it should be obvious what your next move is."

Tessa nodded. "Totally obvious! Go ahead, Cammie. Tell her."

"Uh . . . I would if I knew. Nate?"

My cousin shook his head. "For once, there is something I don't know. What's our next move, Granny?"

"You're going to visit Toni Alfredo-Chin at the embassy on Sunday anyway," Granny said. "What if we make an appointment for you to interview Mr. Valenteen at the same time?"

CHAPTER TWENTY-TWO

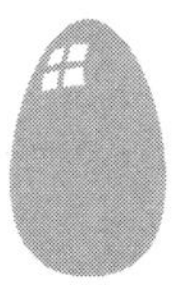

Granny made a phone call.

The appointment was set for three o'clock Sunday at the embassy.

After that it was time for dinner. And guess what—something unusual and amazing happened: Tessa and I got to eat with both our parents! More amazing yet, after dinner, we all watched a movie together.

It was a lot like being a normal family . . . except the food was cooked by the White House chef and served by a butler. And the movie was a brand-new Disney one screened in the private White House theater.

Before bed, we played Monopoly in the solarium. Monopoly is a family tradition on Friday nights, but a lot of times Mom is too busy.

In case you're wondering, the whole time, we hardly talked about the missing dinosaur egg. Nate was with his mom, and Tessa's and my brains needed a break.

What we talked about instead were relaxing topics—

like world peace and pollution and whether the old Disney movies are better than the new ones.

Mom won at Monopoly, which was good because she is a grumpy loser. The rule is loser puts the game away, which is what Tessa and I were doing when Mom's phone rang. She listened, frowned, shrugged and said, "Okay, then. We'll find out more tomorrow, I guess."

When she hung up, she looked at Tessa and me.

"What?" we asked at the same time.

"I am sorry to report that your interview with Mr. Valenteen has been canceled. It seems President Alfredo-Chin has asked him to return home. About an hour ago, he left on a plane bound for the capital of a certain nearby nation."

Can I tell you a secret?

I wasn't that upset that the interview was canceled. With Easter on Sunday and the egg roll on Monday, my family had a lot going on.

Maybe Tessa, Nate and I could just chill until Mr. Morgan and Mr. Webb came back from Pittsburgh. Didn't we already have enough to report?

After we got into bed and turned the lights out, I confessed this to Tessa.

She said, "You're right, Cammie. Mr. Morgan and Mr. Webb probably got the rest of the evidence they need in Pittsburgh, anyway. And now they'll be able to prove it was Professor Bohn all along."

"Wait!" I rolled over. "No! Not Professor Bohn—Mr. Valenteen! Or maybe Professor Rexington."

"Okay, fine," Tessa said, "but you know what Aunt Jen says: 'If you want something done right, you have to do it yourself.'"

I sighed. "So you're saying we don't get the weekend off?"

It was dark in our room, but from the way her sheets rustled, I knew my sister was getting all dramatic the way she does. "What I'm *saying* is: Don't worry about a thing because—lucky for you—I am about to hatch a foolproof plan!"

CHAPTER TWENTY-THREE

There was no time to talk about plans on Saturday morning. As usual, Granny took Tessa to ballet, and Dad went with me to my soccer game. I play for the D.C. Destroyers, and that day we got D.C. Destroyed.

Luckily, unlike some people I could mention, I am not a grumpy loser.

Granny made us sandwiches for lunch. We ate in the Family Kitchen. This was the first chance Tessa and I had had to tell Nate that the interview with Mr. Valenteen had been canceled.

"No worries, though," said Tessa. "I have a foolproof plan!"

"What is it?"

"I'll tell you tomorrow," Tessa said. "Right now, it still needs time to incubate."

"Very funny," said Nate.

Tessa giggled. "I know. Sometimes I crack myself up. Get it?"

When lunch was over, Nate went upstairs to meet

his math tutor. Aunt Jen says Nate's not challenged by fifth-grade math, so he's learning trigonometry. Did I mention how it's lucky Aunt Jen isn't my mom? Meanwhile, I was thinking I might invite my friend Courtney to come over and go bowling—the White House has its own bowling alley—but before I could, Mom came in.

"Mama!" Tessa hopped up and hugged her around the waist. "Are you taking the afternoon off to play with us?"

"I wish I could," Mom said. "But actually, I'm here because Ms. Ann Major has a project, and she needs your help."

Ms. Ann Major is a deputy assistant press secretary on my mom's staff. We know her because her beagle, Pickles, went to obedience school with Hooligan.

"What project?" I asked.

"Ms. Major wants to help us make sure the news guys cover your visit to Toni's house tomorrow," Mom said. "If they do, it will be good for the friendship between our government and President Alfredo-Chin's."

"I'm confused, Mama," Tessa said. "Eb Ghanamamma doesn't like President Alfredo-Chin, right? And Eb Ghanamamma wants democracy. Don't we want democracy, too?"

"Of course we do," Mom said, "but not just yet."

"So what does Ms. Major want us to do?" Tessa asked.

Mom looked at her watch. "Meet her at her desk in ten minutes, and she'll tell you."

* * *

Ms. Major's desk is in a maze of cubicles in the West Wing—which is a building next to the house part of the White House. You get there through a special kind of hallway called a colonnade. Charlotte came, too, and the three of us scrunched into chairs.

The project turned out to be a short video about Tessa's and my friendship with Toni. Right now, Ms. Major wanted us to talk about how great Toni is in front of a camera. Tomorrow at the embassy, somebody would record more footage. Then Ms. Major would edit the clips together for the Web and TV.

If we were lucky, Jan and Larry might even show it.

Tessa said, *"Yes!"* and I said, "Do I have to?"

Ms. Major laughed at me. "It will be painless, I promise."

"Only"—Tessa frowned down at her clothes—"I look like a *wreck*!"

"You both look fine," Ms. Major said. "Come on outside."

We went out to the Rose Garden, where Ms. Major sat Tessa and me down in patio chairs, told us to act natural and aimed the video camera. Tessa straightened her shoulders, tossed her blond curls, flashed her teeth and told the camera who Toni is, how we gave her a puppy named Ozzabelle, and how she is just the greatest friend ever.

I sat like a lump until Ms. Major said, "Cameron? I'm sure you don't realize it, but you're scowling."

I said, "That wasn't a scowl. *This* is a scowl," and showed her.

Ms. Major laughed. "Okay, how about this? Think about successfully solving a mystery."

I must have smiled then, because Ms. Major said, "Better." Then she asked me to tell how we met Toni, and I did, and then—at last—we were done.

Ms. Major had been right. It wasn't that bad. But one thing was for sure. No way was I ever going to watch the finished product.

CHAPTER TWENTY-FOUR

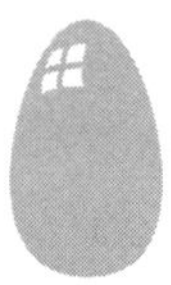

I had been wondering if Easter morning in the White House would be a lot different than Easters in our old house in Northwest Washington.

There were a couple of differences. The main one was that Granny, Aunt Jen and Nate hadn't lived with us back then, so the celebration was bigger now. Also, in the White House, my Easter basket was hidden in an unusual and historic place: under the big bed in the Lincoln Bedroom.

Other than that, Tessa and I put on new dresses, went to church, sang "Alleluia," came home, and ate French toast for brunch—just like we always had.

After brunch, Tessa, Nate and I changed out of our church clothes to go visit Toni. We were going early so we would be back in plenty of time for Easter dinner, which would be served downstairs in the big dining room.

All this time, Tessa still hadn't told me and Nate her plan. But when she got dressed, she put on the pink spangled ball cap she wears for detecting. Then, when we were finally leaving, she said, "Got your notebook, Cammie? You're going to need it."

The embassy of a certain nearby nation is in an old brick building in Georgetown, about fifteen minutes from the White House. There is a curlicued black metal fence around the building. In the front is a door leading to offices, and around a corner is a door that goes to the residence, where Toni and her family live.

When Malik pulled the van up to the curb, there were already white TV trucks parked there and news guys with cameras and microphones clustered on the sidewalk.

Hooligan was in the back of our van, so I walked around, opened his crate, attached his leash to his collar and let him out. It was Tessa's job to carry an Easter basket the White House pastry chef had prepared for Toni and her family.

"Ready?" Granny looked at Tessa, me and Nate. "All right then, let's do this."

Standing on each side of the embassy gate were soldiers in dark blue uniforms and caps. They had guns on their belts and bigger guns slung over their shoulders. I smiled at one as we walked through, but he didn't smile back.

Yikes, I thought, but then I remembered that Secret Service people would be all around as long as we were inside. There was nothing to worry about—even if the soldiers from the nearby nation didn't seem so friendly.

We followed a walkway to the front door, and Granny rang the doorbell. Instantly, there was a total ruckus of hysterical yip-yip-yipping from inside.

Hooligan responded with woof-woof-woofing of his own, not to mention he pulled the leash so hard I had to brace myself. Granny offered to take it, because she's heavier, which would have been a good idea, except just then the door opened and here came Ozzabelle busting out at the same time Hooligan tried to bust in and—*bam!*—there was a drooling, fur-flying doggy collision.

Meanwhile, the leash dropped and—a few spins and tumbles later—both dogs were racing in circles around the brick courtyard while all the grown-ups either scurried out of the way or yelled or both.

In the background, I heard shouting from the news guys—"Great stuff!" "Are you getting this?"—and the whir and click of their equipment.

One thing Tessa, Nate and I have learned about doggy behavior: scurrying and yelling doesn't help. Tessa held the Easter basket up high, but besides that we just stayed out of the way and watched. Then Toni came outside and grinned at us and shouted, "Hello!"

The canine chaos was settling down—Granny had hold of Hooligan's leash, and Malik had cornered Ozzabelle—when my nose told me someone else had come out of the house, someone who smelled like perfume and cigarettes. I figured it had to be Toni's grandmother, and I turned around... and got the shock of my life.

It was the lady with black hair from the security video at Mega Bird Farm!

CHAPTER TWENTY-FIVE

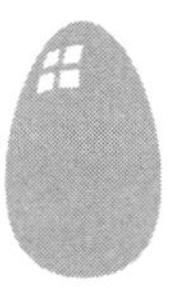

My heart went *thump*, and I nudged Tessa—who looked around, too, and then so did Nate.

I don't think the lady liked how surprised we looked, because she quickly disappeared back into the house. At the same time, her frown had given me goose bumps. Was she really Toni's grandmother?

It was a few minutes before I found out. During that time, the dogs were taken to the backyard to play, and the news guys shot photos and video of my family, the Easter basket and Toni.

"Doesn't your grandmother want to be in the pictures?" Granny asked Toni.

"Oh, no." Toni shook her head. "She does not like the publicity. She says it is not her 'style.'"

Eventually, Granny and Malik left to go back to the White House. The plan was for them to return to pick us up in a couple of hours. Nate, Tessa and I followed Toni inside. In the foyer, a small, gray-haired woman greeted us with hugs—Toni's grandmother. She smelled like soap.

"It is my pleasure to meet Antonia's dear friends," she said. "And I must also take this opportunity to thank you for giving us the little dog, Ozzabelle. She is a nuisance, but she makes me laugh."

Toni's house was fancy—lots of shiny brass and black paint. Toni led us up the marble stairs to her room, which was big like Tessa's and mine. It had a bed and also a sofa, chairs and a table. I noticed the rock collection right away because it was lit up on a shelf over a desk.

Before we sat down, Toni put on some music. After a few seconds, I realized it was familiar—Eb Ghanamamma! But that couldn't be right. Wasn't Eb Ghanamamma protesting against Toni's very own uncle, President Manfred Alfredo-Chin?

I wanted to ask about that, but I was afraid it would be rude. And I wanted to ask about the lady with the black hair, too. But how was I supposed to explain where I'd seen her?

So I kept quiet.

But Tessa didn't.

"Get out your notebook, Cammie," she said as soon as we sat down. Then she straightened her detecting hat, crossed her arms over her chest and gave Toni the steely look she uses when she's questioning a suspect.

Uh-oh—was this Tessa's foolproof plan? But Toni wasn't a suspect! Toni was our friend!

I started to shake my head at Tessa, but Toni said, "Oh, good, are you planning now to ask questions relating to a certain mystery? Because that is in reality the reason I invited you here today."

Tessa said, "Antonia Alfredo-Chin, who is that lady with the black hair who is not your grandmother, anyway?"

Toni nodded. "That is an easy question. This woman is a new housekeeper. She and my *abuelita* came to Washington from our nation together a couple of months ago. She is not very good at her job, and she does not smile. But why—?"

Tessa held up her hand. "If you don't mind, I am asking the questions here."

I closed my eyes and shook my head. Oh, Tessa.

But Toni giggled. "This is like a real detective show! What else do you want to know from me?"

"Why did your new housekeeper go to Mega Bird Farm this week to ask if Mr. Valenteen bought an ostrich egg there last week that he took to the National Museum of Natural History pretending to be from a delivery company that for real does not even *exist*?"

Toni looked at Tessa. Then she looked at Nate and me. "Huh?" she said.

Tessa said, "Okay, we can come back to that one. How about this? How well do you know this Mr. Valenteen guy from your nation? The one Hooligan knocked over on TV?"

Toni said, "Not well, but it is said he sometimes does

secret projects for my uncle, President Alfredo-Chin. It may be possible that he is a *spy*."

Nate and I looked at each other. *A spy?*

And Tessa said, "Aha! So when Mr. Valenteen took the ostrich egg to the museum—was that a special project for President Alfredo-Chin? Like a *spy* project?"

Toni didn't answer, but Nate nodded like he had just figured something out. "I see what you're getting at, Tessa! You think the idea was to embarrass Professor Bohn and Professor Rexington at their talk—make it seem like they're so dumb they can't tell the difference between an ostrich egg and a dinosaur egg. Then—if the professors were wrong and there was no dinosaur egg—the old legend could still be true, and President Alfredo-Chin could stay president in perpetuity!"

"Exactly," Tessa said, even though I know my sister, and I could tell she had never thought all that one bit.

Toni still didn't say anything. Instead, she got up and walked over to her rock collection. "I do not know about ostrich eggs, but I do know many people in my nation disbelieve that silly legend, and many people are in favor of democracy." She turned to face us. "That is why now, if you don't mind, I would like to show you something."

Toni's collection included a white geode, a purple amethyst, a lump of turquoise and two pieces of pyrite, also known as fool's gold. But the rock she brought over for us to look at wasn't pretty like those. It was gray and boring and oval-shaped. She held it out...

. . . and my heart almost stopped for the second time in an hour.

Tessa had turned pale, and her voice squeaked. “Is that what I think it is?”

“Yes,” said Toni. “It is the missing dinosaur egg fossil from the National Museum.”

CHAPTER TWENTY-SIX

Tessa's color came back fast.

"*Woot!* Cammie—get Mr. Morgan and Mr. Webb on the phone! The First Kids have solved another one! And Toni"—she looked at our friend sorrowfully—"I hate to tell you, but you are under arrest. Now—give over that dinosaur egg you stole!"

Tessa made a grab, which caused Toni to squeal and jump back.

"Oh, for gosh sake, Tessa, would you chill?" I said. "We are not arresting anybody. If Toni ever stole any egg, would she invite us over to see it?"

Tessa pouted. "Oh, *fine.* But, Toni, if you're not a thief, how did you get hold of a missing dinosaur egg?"

Toni shook her head. "I wish I knew. But the truth is it simply appeared in my rock collection."

Tessa crossed her arms over her chest again. "And when was that?"

"It was Thursday, one week ago. I had just said my prayers that night, and I looked up at my collection and saw it. I had seen the picture on Jan and Larry, so I knew immediately what it was."

I was scribbling as fast as I could and trying to think at the same time. Thursday was the same day the dinosaur egg's crate was scanned at the airport here in Washington, the same day Mr. Valenteen bought the ostrich egg at Mega Bird Farm and the same day Mr. Valenteen—pretending to be Red Heart Delivery—took the ostrich egg to the museum.

Just in case, I asked Toni if she had ever heard of Red Heart Delivery, and she said, "Yes! I saw a van with that name on our street. I noticed because I wondered if they only delivered flowers and chocolate and diamonds."

"When was that?" Tessa asked.

Toni frowned. "It was that same Thursday. I remember I was still wearing my clothes from horseback riding—and my lessons are on Thursday."

Tessa nodded. "So Mr. Valenteen must've replaced the dinosaur egg with an ostrich egg and brought the dinosaur egg here. After that, he must've brought it upstairs to put in Toni's collection."

Toni shook her head. "No, no—only the family and our guests may come upstairs in the residence! Mr. Valenteen would never be allowed."

"In that case, he gave it to somebody, and *they* brought it upstairs," Nate said. "But why? And who did he give it to?"

"It cannot have been my father," Toni said, "because he was away last week. But wait—I am forgetting.

There is the housekeeper, Mrs. Casera. She is permitted upstairs because of course she must do the cleaning."

"There you go," said Tessa. "I think Mr. Valenteen was working with Mrs. Casera, and he gave the egg to her."

I thought that might be right. "But why did she put it in Toni's rock collection?"

"And if Mrs. Casera was working with Mr. Valenteen," said Nate, "why did she have to go back to Mega Bird Farm to ask about the ostrich egg? There's something we're not getting here."

I thought of how Mrs. Casera and Toni's *abuelita* looked a little bit alike. "Toni," I said, "did Mr. Valenteen know your grandmother by sight? Or Mrs. Casera?"

Toni shrugged. "Perhaps not. As I told you, my abuelita does not like publicity, so she rarely appears on TV or in magazines."

"Then maybe," I said, thinking out loud, "Mr. Valenteen was supposed to give the egg to Mrs. Casera, and she was supposed to get rid of it—all to preserve the legend for President Alfredo-Chin. But instead, Mr. Valenteen gave the egg to your grandmother."

Toni said, "You mean it was a case of mistaken identity!"

I nodded. "And Mrs. Casera—when she didn't get the egg like she was supposed to—she went to Mega Bird Farm to check up."

"If you are right, it was my abuelita who put the egg in my rock collection," Toni said. "Maybe she did not know what it was, or maybe she did know and wanted a hiding place. . . .”

Tessa jumped up. “Well, what are we waiting for? Let’s go ask her!”

Toni remained seated. “If I may—there is something more important right now even than solving this mystery. You see, I asked you here today for a particular reason. I believe the First Kids are the only people in the world who can help me do what is right. We must return the dinosaur egg to its rightful owners at the museum, but we must do this without embarrassing my uncle, my father or anyone else from my nation. Is this possible? Will you help me?”

CHAPTER TWENTY-SEVEN

Nate and I looked at each other. We wanted to help—but how?

Tessa's reaction was different. She sat back down, rubbed her hands together and said: "*No problemo!* All we have to do is think sneaky. And thinking sneaky is one of my talents."

Nate nodded. "True."

And the way it turned out—Tessa was right. After about five minutes of brainstorming, she had added up one dinosaur egg, one Easter basket and one big Monday event at the White House to equal one foolproof plan.

"All we need now," she said in conclusion, "is chocolate chips."

Toni nodded. "There are plenty in the kitchen. But we must hurry! Your grandmother will be back in only one hour."

The kitchen in the residence part of the embassy is on the first floor and not that different from one in a normal house. When we walked in—luckily—no one was there. Toni went straight to a pantry cupboard and pulled out the chocolate chips. From another cupboard, she got a pan.

Then she poured the chips into the pan and turned on the stove.

"You've got to stir it, or they'll burn," I said.

"Who cares?" Tessa said. "It's not like anybody's going to eat it—*owieee!* Think of your teeth!"

"No, no one's going to eat it—but burnt chocolate smells terrible," I said. "Someone might come to investigate."

"Investigate what?" said a voice from the doorway—Toni's abuelita!

Now we had a puzzle. Did we tell her what we were doing? Ask her about the dinosaur egg—whether she had put it in Toni's collection, whether she knew what it was?

But what if she tried to stop us from returning it to Dr. Bohn and Dr. Rexington at the museum?

For a moment, we all froze. Then Toni turned and said—a little too cheerfully—"*Hello, Abuelita!* Uh... we were just making some, uh—"

"Easter treats!" My sneaky sister helped her out, and—without us kids even talking about it—the decision was made.

Abuelita raised her eyebrows. "Oh, yes? That is very nice."

"Abuelita," Toni said, thinking fast, "would you mind getting the beautiful Easter basket brought to me this afternoon by my friends? Only . . . I am sorry, but I am not sure where I put it. Perhaps in the parlor? Or my bedroom?"

Abuelita said certainly, she didn't mind looking, and was barely out the door when the three of us rushed to the stove. The chocolate had melted by now. It was smooth and glossy and smelled delicious—but we couldn't get sidetracked with a taste test. We had dipping to do.

It might be that someday you'll have to dip a dinosaur egg fossil in chocolate to disguise it, and if so, I have some advice:

1) Use tongs.
2) Dip repeatedly.
3) Have plenty of paper towels handy.
4) Decorate with sprinkles.

By the time Toni's grandmother found the Easter basket, our Easter egg of unusual size was chilling in the freezer, and—if I do say so myself—for a rock, it looked good. We thanked Toni's grandmother, then took the beautiful basket apart—which seemed a little sad. The nice chocolate eggs and cookies we put in a bowl for Toni's family. The Easter grass and a few jelly beans we left.

Later we would put our special chocolate egg in the center and walk right out of the embassy with it.

At least, that was the plan.

"And the Easter treats you made, may I see?" Abuelita asked.

Uh-oh.

I was worried, but Toni went straight over to the freezer and opened it. Would the disguise be successful?

Abuelita studied the egg. Then she looked at us...and for a split second, I was terrified she knew exactly what we were up to. But she couldn't, could she?

Still, it was a relief when she smiled and said, "Such a large piece of chocolate!"

Score! So far, Tessa's sneaky plan was working perfectly!

CHAPTER TWENTY-EIGHT

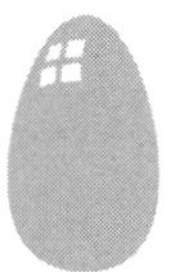

While the chocolate-dipped dinosaur egg finished cooling, Toni, Tessa, Nate and I went out and played Frisbee with the dogs. It was almost time for Granny to pick us up when we went back inside and packed the egg into the basket.

We were admiring our work when Abuelita came into the kitchen to say the White House van was out front.

That was when I thought of those unsmiling soldiers at the gate and realized maybe this wouldn't be so easy. None of us had ever tried to sneak a dinosaur egg fossil out of an embassy before. We didn't know what it would be like.

In the front hall, Abuelita gave us each a hug good-bye.

Then, with Tessa in the lead, Toni, Nate and I walked out the front door and around to the courtyard. At the same time, a woman from the embassy staff brought

Hooligan from the back. Since I was carrying the Easter basket, Nate took Hooligan's leash.

Through the black metal fence, I saw the White House van parked on the street. Also outside were two Secret Service guys. Jeremy was one, and I didn't know the other.

"Good-bye, dear friends." Toni gave us each a kiss on the cheek. When it was my turn she whispered, "And good luck!"

Toni is super pretty, and even though I was busy worrying, I noticed that her kiss made Nate turn pink.

We started walking toward the gate, and the soldier on the left unlatched it. With the dinosaur egg inside, the Easter basket was heavy and awkward to carry. I felt like every step was an effort, but I kept my chin tilted up so I would look confident.

Step, step, step, step, step. We were almost out...

...but then, in an instant, everything changed. The soldier on the left—responding to something he heard on the earpiece of his radio—shoved the metal gate shut—*clank!*—and now our way was blocked.

I froze. Outside the fence, Jeremy and the other Secret Service agent squared their shoulders and rocked back on their heels, ready for anything. Meanwhile, Malik emerged from the White House van.

Toni spoke to the soldier: "What is wrong? Open the gate at once!"

The soldier answered, "Your friends may leave, Miss Alfredo-Chin. But the holiday basket must remain."

Toni stamped her foot. "The basket is my gift to them!"

"I have my orders," he said. "Once the basket has been returned to Mrs. Casera, then your friends may leave."

Mrs. Casera—wha...? But then I smelled her cigarette smoke and turned. Out of nowhere, she had appeared beside me. Scowling, she reached for the Easter basket.

I have never been so scared, and—in case you don't know—I am not a brave person. But the egg was important to science, it didn't belong to her and—darn it—we had gone to a lot of trouble to get it back.

So instead of handing it over, I held it closer, stepped away and shook my head no.

Hooligan growled.

For a few seconds, it looked like a standoff—our team vs their team. The numbers were about equal, but their soldiers had way bigger guns.

Then Abuelita appeared in the courtyard. "Let the children pass, Sergeant."

"We have our orders, ma'am," he said.

"Orders?" she repeated. "From whom are these orders? I am the mother of the president of our nation and the mother of the ambassador!"

The soldier looked uncertain until Mrs. Casera spoke up. "His orders are from me."

"A *housekeeper*?" Abuelita said.

Mrs. Casera made an awful face she probably

thought was a smile. "I'm afraid that was only a cover. I am in fact a high official in the secret police force of our nation, sent here to ensure the security of the embassy."

Abuelita nodded. "Ah, I see. This explains why you are such a terrible housekeeper."

Mrs. Casera ignored the insult and grabbed the handle of the basket. To protect me, Hooligan lunged, which made Mrs. Casera shriek and let go, and after that things really got crazy. The sound of radio static and shouting voices filled the air. Ozzabelle showed up to yip and run in circles.

"Throw the basket over the fence, Cammie!" Tessa called, but the basket was way too heavy. Meanwhile, three men in suits, taking orders from Mrs. Casera, advanced toward me—and I was trapped!

It was Ozzabelle who came to my rescue, zigzagging between my feet and snapping at the men, who tried to stomp her with their shiny shoes. No way would Hooligan allow that! Protecting his little buddy, he jumped and threw his full furry weight against the first man, who fell against the second, who fell against the third, so that they all went over like dominoes.

Outside the fence, Jeremy was on his radio. Maybe Mom would send in the marines to rescue us! But if that got on the news, it would not look good for the friendship between the United States and a nearby nation.

My thoughts were as chaotic as the action around me, when all of a sudden, everything changed—like someone had hit the Pause button. First the soldiers at the gate turned their heads, then the three men in suits on the ground, then Abuelita and even the dogs.

They were looking at someone standing in one of the second-floor windows—and when finally Mrs. Casera looked up, too, she groaned in dismay.

The man in the window was wearing a blue work shirt. He had curly black hair, dark eyes, a crooked nose and a skinny face. His expression wasn't pouty like it is on his CDs, though. It was stern.

"Wait a second, that's—" I started to say, but Toni shushed me with a finger to her lips. When I looked again, the man was gone.

Tessa took advantage of the momentary confusion: "Run, Cammie!"

I did, and I could tell that now the soldiers didn't know what to do. Obey Abuelita? Obey Mrs. Casera?

Tessa crossed her arms over her chest and spoke to them: "It looks like you just have to decide for yourselves. Whose side are you on?"

CHAPTER TWENTY-NINE

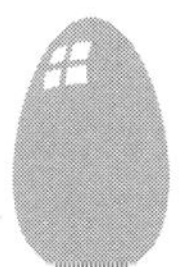

For a moment, the soldier on the left looked hopeless and confused, but then his face changed. He had made his decision.

"You'll pay for this, Sergeant!" cried Mrs. Casera as he unlatched the gate and let us through.

"Thanks very much, Sergeant!" said Tessa. Then she shoved me ahead, and Nate and Hooligan followed. Before I knew what was happening, Granny had hustled us into the White House van and Malik was gunning the motor.

"Are you okay?" Granny asked. "And wherever did you get such a huge chocolate egg for your Easter basket?"

"We're fine," I said, breathing for what seemed like the first time in a while.

"But we can't tell you about the egg, Granny," said Tessa.

"We promised," said Nate.

"Hmph," said Granny. "Perhaps we will discuss the

egg later. For now, though, I have to tell you Easter dinner will be delayed. There are a couple of gentlemen waiting in the Treaty Room to see you."

It was Mr. Morgan and Mr. Webb in the Treaty Room—I mean, in case you hadn't figured that out. Mom was there, too, making a special guest appearance. So was Charlotte.

"Hey, hi—how was Pittsburgh?" Tessa asked when we'd all sat down. "We have bad news, though," she went on. "Professor Bohn didn't do it."

Mr. Morgan nodded. "We know. We established that the first day. So right after we sent you the postcard, we left Pittsburgh to travel to a certain nearby nation."

"Wait, what?" I said. "Why didn't you tell us?"

Mr. Morgan looked at Mom, and Mom said, "I'm afraid their trip was top secret."

"Oh, *fine*," said Tessa. "So you knew about it and didn't tell us!"

"I'm sorry," Mom said, and that was all. One thing I'm finding out—when your mom is the president, there are a lot of things she can't tell you.

"I bet we know some things that you don't," Tessa said—and you could practically hear the *nyah-nyah-nyah* in her voice. "Like how the housekeeper is an officer in the police and Mr. Valenteen is a *spy*."

Mr. Morgan and Mr. Webb looked at each other. "How did *you*—"

Tessa waved her arms the way she does. "Never mind. And we've got another secret, too, so don't even bother asking where the dinosaur egg is now, because we won't tell you."

Mr. Morgan said, "You know where the dinosaur egg is?"

Mom looked equally surprised, which—I have to admit—kind of made me feel a little *nyah-nyah-nyah* myself.

Tessa said, "I never said we knew where the egg was."

And Nate said, "But if we did, we'd for sure turn it over to the scientists it belongs to, the ones who want to study it."

"And now we have some questions for *you*, Mr. Morgan and Mr. Webb." Tessa crossed her arms over her chest. "At the embassy today, there was a guy in the window, and when he showed up, it was like he was a rock star or something. All of a sudden, the soldiers didn't know who to listen to."

Nate started to say, "Wasn't the guy in the window Eb—"

But Mr. Webb put a finger to his lips, and Mom said, "It will be better for everyone if we don't name names. I will only say this. There is a hero of the protest movement in a certain nearby nation who is beloved by the people there. It is even possible he will one day be elected to office. It is also possible that, for his own safety, he must remain in hiding for now. Who knows? He may even be in hiding in his nation's embassy in the United States—protected by relatives of the current president."

All of a sudden, things started to make sense.

"If that's true," I said, "maybe President Manfred Alfredo-Chin sent a high official in the secret police to find this guy...and maybe she didn't do such a good job?"

Mom nodded. "Maybe."

"Wow." Tessa shook her head. "So sometimes politics are so complicated even people in the same family disagree with each other! I'm sure glad it's not like that here."

"Not in our family, at least," Mom said. "And now that you three are safe and sound, the important thing is the egg. It must be returned as quietly as possible. And it looks to me like the First Kids are on the case."

CHAPTER THIRTY

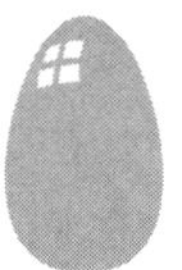

The morning of the Easter egg roll was clear and bright. The party started at nine-thirty with "the President's Own" United States Marine Band playing "Here Comes Peter Cottontail," and Hooligan—trying to look dignified—making an appearance on the Truman Balcony wearing pink-and-white bunny ears.

Later, singers and dancers performed, and authors and actors and senators read stories. Nate played the piano—a song called "Easter Parade" by a man named Irving Berlin.

Meanwhile, Tessa and I got to roll Easter eggs with kids. I like the really little kids best because they don't understand we're supposed to be famous, and they just act normal.

All the time, though, what Tessa, Nate and I were really looking forward to was meeting one special guest, Professor Cordell Bohn.

We had an Easter basket to give him.

With all those people, we couldn't count on running

into Professor Bohn, so we made arrangements to meet him near the East Gate at noon.

"There he is." Tessa pointed. Nate was carrying the basket. I waved, and Professor Bohn waved back. When we got closer, I saw that his usually merry face looked sad.

"I have to go back to Pittsburgh tomorrow," he said. "It's been a tough time here in Washington. I don't think Professor Rexington is ever going to forgive me for letting the dinosaur egg get away."

Tessa consulted her Barbie watch, the one she's too old for. "In about thirty seconds," she said, "you are going to feel a whole lot better. But first I have one question. How come you called Jan and Larry to tell them the egg was missing? To certain people I won't name, that looked suspicious."

Professor Bohn raised his eyebrows. "I called because I wanted to get the word out," he said. "I thought if it was on the news, a lot of people would hear about it and someone might call the police with a tip. But"—he looked at each of us in turn—"I don't get it. *Why* am I going to feel better?"

"Because we have a present for you." Nate held out the basket.

Professor Bohn started to say, "Aw, you didn't have to—" but then he wasn't expecting the basket to be so heavy and almost dropped it on his foot. "What in the world . . . ?"

"Don't try to eat that egg," Tessa warned him. "Seriously."

The oversized chocolate egg nestled among the jelly beans in the green Easter grass. We had asked the White House pastry chef to add a few pastel frosting flowers that morning, so the egg really did look nice.

Professor Bohn stared down at it, and his jaw dropped. "It's the right size, the right shape, the right weight, but... it can't be!"

"Yeah, it can," Tessa said.

"But this is wonderful!" Professor Bohn said. "I must contact the museum at once. They'll want to make an announcement, and—"

Tessa crossed her arms over her chest. Nate shook his head. My voice was stern: "No, no, no, no, *no*."

"We never gave this to you," Nate said.

"It just appeared, you don't know how," said Tessa. "It's a matter of national security."

"But still—good luck with your research," I said.

"And"—Tessa wagged her finger—"be sure to share with Professor Rexington! Even though you think she's wrong about how the dinosaur's related to the birds and all, scientists have to play fair just like everybody else."

THE WHITE HOUSE EASTER EGG ROLL

First Kid Tessa Parks can be forgiven for thinking an eggroll is something you eat at a Chinese restaurant. An eggroll really is a Chinese-style appetizer. Less well known is an egg roll—two words—a game in which competitors use a serving spoon to push eggs across a lawn. The tradition of egg rolling around Eastertime comes from England and is still popular in some places there.

With one exception, egg rolling is not so common in the United States. But that exception is a big one: the White House Easter Egg Roll, which takes place the Monday after Easter.

HISTORY

While some people say it was First Lady Dolley Madison who started the egg roll tradition in Washington, there is no proof of this. In fact, the first recorded egg-rolling activities there seem to have been spontaneous. After the Civil War, children enjoyed rolling hard-boiled eggs from their lunch pails on the slopes outside the Capitol in the spring. The local newspapers wrote about this, also noting approvingly that these children playing together were from all races and classes.

That kind of integration was unusual in nineteenth-century Washington. As a side note, you would have to fast-forward all the way to 1953, when Mamie Eisenhower was First Lady, before African-American children would be invited to attend the official Easter Egg Roll at the White House. More than fifty years after that, President and Mrs. Obama made a point of including same-sex couples and their children on the guest list.

The Easter tradition moved to the White House in 1878. That spring, Congress had outlawed games of any kind on the Capitol grounds to save the lawn. President Rutherford B. Hayes learned how disappointed local children were one evening when he was taking a walk. According to Hayes's journal, a boy approached him and shouted, "Say! Say! Are you going to let us roll eggs in your yard?"

The surprised president was from Ohio and didn't know about the local tradition. When his staff explained, he and his wife, Lucy, decided that yes, they would let the boy—and all the other children of the town—roll eggs on the White House lawn. Thus the White House Easter Egg Roll was born.

BUSINESS OPPORTUNITIES

By 1889, when Benjamin Harrison was president, the event was so well established that vendors selling fruit, waffles, peanuts, balloons, pinwheels and sweets set up shop outside the White House gates to serve the people waiting in line.

The vendors weren't the only ones who saw the egg roll as a business opportunity. Since adults were not allowed to attend without children, clever kids figured out they could get paid for escorting childless adults. Once on the grounds, the children doubled back to wait for their next customer. During the Great Depression of the 1930s, an eleven-year-old boy told a reporter the five quarters he earned that day would help pay his family's rent.

THE TROUBLE WITH EGGS

While the Easter Egg Roll has always been a hit with kids, it has not always been popular with the First Family. President Theodore Roosevelt's wife, Edith, wanted to call it off entirely because it was hard on the lawn and she didn't like the smell of leftover eggs. First Lady Pat Nixon had the same problem when she tried using hard-boiled eggs for an old-fashioned Easter egg hunt. The eggs that weren't found remained rotting outside for days—*pew!*

President Gerald Ford tried using plastic eggs, but it was President and Mrs. Ronald Reagan who came up with the most enduring solution: painted wooden eggs. Now thousands of colorful wooden eggs, stamped with the president's and First Lady's signatures, are given away every year as keepsakes.

Mrs. Reagan can claim an additional egg roll distinction. She not only hosted the event when her husband was president in the 1980s, but she also attended as a guest of President and Mrs. Calvin Coolidge when she was a child during the 1920s.

PRESIDENTIAL PETS

As a guest in 1927, the future First Lady might have seen the glamorous Grace Coolidge parading among the partygoers, carrying one of the best-known White House pets, Rebecca Raccoon. At the 1922 event, President Warren G. Harding's photogenic Airedale, Laddie Boy, sniffed kids, shook hands and did tricks. Eleanor Roosevelt brought first dogs Meggie, a Scottie, and Major, a German shepherd, to the 1933 egg roll.

Like the fictional Hooligan in *The Case of the Missing Dinosaur Egg*, the Obamas' Portuguese water dog, Bo, has appeared wearing pink-and-white bunny ears—and looking slightly embarrassed. Since the Nixon administration in the 1970s, the Easter Bunny himself has also stopped in, usually played by a White House staff member.

THE EGG ROLL TODAY

Today, in spite of the name, egg rolling is only a small part of what goes on at the annual event, which attracts about 35,000 people. Activities may include basketball, tennis and yoga, as well as cooking demonstrations and storytelling by celebrities. In recent years, J. K. Rowling has read from her Harry Potter books, President Barack Obama has read *Where the Wild Things Are* by Maurice Sendak, and actress Reese Witherspoon has read *The Best Pet of All* by David LaRochelle.

Among recent performers are Justin Bieber, Fergie, and the cast of *Glee*. On hand since 1889 has been "The President's Own" United States Marine Band, whose repertoire includes a John Philip Sousa song called "Easter Monday on the White House Lawn."

Most of the guests at the White House Easter Egg Roll get tickets through a free lottery conducted online. If you want to try your luck, go to www.recreation.gov to sign up a few weeks before Easter, usually early in March. In 2012, about one in eight people who wanted tickets got them. To keep the crowds manageable, guests are assigned a time slot and permitted to stay only about ninety minutes.

If you want more information on the White House Easter Egg Roll today, a good source is www.whitehouse.gov. For more on the event's history, check out a great article by C. L. Arbelbide in the spring 2000 *Prologue*, a publication of the National Archives, "With Easter Monday, You Get Egg Roll at the White House." It is also available online at www.archives.gov.